C000062249

INFINITY

## ISSUE 31: SUMMER 2022

**Award-winning science fiction magazine
published in Scotland for the Universe.**

We're supporting

and we thank Cymera for supporting us.

ISSN: 2059-2590
ISBN: 978-1-7396736-2-8

Submissions of fiction, art, reviews, poetry, non-fiction are
welcomed: visit the website to find out how to submit.

www.shorelineofinfinity.com
Publisher
Shoreline of Infinity Publications / The New Curiosity Shop
Edinburgh
Scotland
230522

Cover art: Stref

# Contents

## Editorial Team

*Co-founder, Editor-in-Chief, Editor:*
Noel Chidwick

*Co-founder:* Mark Toner

*Deputy Editor & Poetry Editor:*
Russell Jones

*Fiction Editor:* Eris Young

*Reviews Editor:* Ann Landmann

*Non-fiction Editor:* Pippa Goldschmidt

*Art Director:* Mark Toner

*Marketing & Publicity Editor:*
Yasmin Kanaan

*Production Editor:* James T Harding

*Copy-editors:* Pippa Goldschmidt,
Russell Jones, Iain Maloney, Eris
Young, Cat Hellisen

*Proof Reader:* Yasmin Kanaan

*Fiction Consultant:* Eric Brown

## First Contact

www.shorelineofinfinity.com

contact@shorelineofinfinity.com

*Twitter:* @shoreinf

# Pull up a Log

## Many Multiverses

**'sfunny how themes** come along in science fiction in waves. In this issue Anna Mocikat asks "is cyberpunk dead?" We could also ask the same question about steampunk – do we pack away our green-glassed goggles in our mahogany dark crates of brass and leather?

Currently, and it's a topic I thoroughly enjoy, we're into multiverses and parallel universes. Cinematically we currently have Dr Strange 2, with a classic Marvel cacophony of fight scenes in colliding universes, and *Everything Everywhere All at Once* which I'm eagerly anticipating. In proper, written-word Science Fiction, Charles Stross has been exploring parallel Earths to great effect in his Merchant Princes series, and neatly side-steps the perils of writing near-future Science Fiction.

Shit, at the moment, the thought that a couple of universes along the shelf there's a better version of this world — or at least one that doesn't feel like it's shooting itself in both feet and barbecuing the results — is worth a few moments of our time.

Ruth EJ Booth takes a keen-eyed wander in this territory in *Noise and Sparks*. Remember the Covid pandemic? Some folk seem to think it's over, but only because they want it to be, so they shift themselves into a universe where it *is* over, apparently, dragging the rest of us behind.

I'm now standing on tippy-toes to see what the next SF theme will be: telepathy, maybe? Anyone care to take on *The Chrysalids*, bring it up to date?

It'll need a label: hands up for 'thinkpunk!'

*Noel Chidwick*
*Editor-in-Chief*
*Shoreline of Infinity*
*June 2022*

5

# Everywhere is Everywhere and Anywhere Else is Nowhere

## Chris Barnham

Inside the house, male voices belt out the fortieth rendition of "Blessing grant, oh God of nations, on the isles of Fiji", sung by the bunch of rugby players who ported in with Alex from Malibu. These guys are built like wardrobes, and they've drunk western LA county dry. Kelly has the French windows open and is working on her fifth large Chardonnay of the afternoon, watching the sun sink into the hills, casting shadows on the river.

When the phone rings, it takes her several seconds to place the sound. She finds the receiver wedged between two cushions of the chesterfield.

"Kelly? It's Byron."

"Byron! How are you? Haven't seen you in…"

Well, how long is it? They kept in touch after college and there was a year when they were an item, but that must be a decade ago. Kelly's hazy about it now, but didn't they part on bad terms? Byron called her a sellout for working in PR; she said he was a loser for thinking there was any money in whatever neuroscience dead-end he was mad about that week.

"Kelly, we need to talk. There's something..."

"Shores of GOLDEN SAND! And sunshine, happiness, and song! Stand UNITED! We of Fiji. Fame and glory ever!" A conga line of Fijian rugby players sashays down the staircase. Alex is at the front, a bottle of rum in one hand, wearing a pair of shorts as a hat. "Kelly!" he yells. "Come to Fiji. The sun's coming up." Kelly shakes her head and points at the phone.

"...important we talk," Byron says. "People need to—"

"ONWARD march TOGETHER!" The rugby singers boom louder as they reach the Port room, but the volume shrinks as they go through. "GOD.... Bless...Fiji."

"I need your help." Byron's voice cracks. "I didn't know who else to call."

The house falls silent as the last reveller transmits to Fiji. Kelly hates a quiet house; it swells with empty space for her thoughts to fill.

"Come over, Byron. But be quick. I've got a date in Fiji."

"I'll be there as soon as I can," he says. "Don't tell anyone. And don't use the -." Kelly clicks off the phone and drops it on the couch.

She waits a whole half hour and Byron doesn't show. She checks the Port settings maybe a hundred times. Kelly hates hanging around, especially when the floating party is ported to the other side of the world. It's dark outside and a Fijian sunrise sounds attractive. She picks up the phone and presses ringback. The call shunts to voicemail and she hangs up.

She changes into a swimsuit and sandals. In the Port room she half-expects Byron to flicker in behind the glass door before she can leave, but the cubicle's dark. She steps inside. The cubicle lights come on and ripple in lilac, and a puff of air on her face makes her blink. When she reopens her eyes, she's in a different room and she's got that tingling buzz of her senses dialled up a notch, like a first glass of wine. People say porting stimulates endorphins; it sure works for Kelly.

She opens the door and smells the sea. This house has wooden floors, smudged with sand and damp footprints. Outside, a verandah gives onto a beach. As always after a Port, Kelly's mildly horny and fuzzy, briefly unsure where she is or why she's here. Down at the shore, people dance around a driftwood fire. A fat sun heaves itself into a salmon sky. Kelly runs to join the party.

After Fiji, she and Alex port to Tokyo for shopping, before a night in a cabin in the Himalayan foothills. They sit outside in canvas chairs and drink raksi with soda.

"I had a call from Byron. Remember him?"

"That wanker. He came over?" Alex is a silhouette against the star-freckled night.

"No. He called. Like, on the phone."

"Scared you'd punch him again?"

"I never punched him." But even as she denies it, Kelly recalls the last time she saw Byron. A London pub, he had a new job and was moving to Leeds. Come with me, he said. Get away from those airheads at the agency. They're my friends, she shouted, and when he grabbed her arm to stop her leaving, she yanked it free and swung the other to deliver an open-handed whack on the side of his head. She didn't look back.

"That him on the phone when the Fijians were there?"

"He sounded worried."

"Worried about what?"

"No idea. He said people needed to know about something. Wanted my help getting the word out."

"You're definitely the girl for that."

9

"It's odd he didn't port in. He said he'd come over, but never turned up."

"Forget him," Alex says. "If he doesn't come, it's not important. Where shall we go tomorrow?"

Kelly knows he's right, but it bothers her. What was the research Byron was working on? She thinks they might have argued about it back then. Alex moves to top up her raksi, but she puts her hand over the cup. Her thoughts are too sluggish for more alcohol.

*I need another port jump. Clear my head.*

It's an odd thought, one she's never had fully formed before, but it's been there at the back of her mind, like the desire for a sharpening gin at the end of the day, or the first cigarette in the morning.

After Nepal, they port to Istanbul for breakfast of dark coffee and freshly baked pastries. They spend the afternoon and evening in Sorrento, where Kelly buys a new dress, and they have pizza and iced white wine in a garden overlooking the Bay of Naples. Clouds caress the summit of Vesuvius, giving the illusion of smoke from the volcano's crater.

They port home late. Kelly's tired and while Alex unpacks, she drifts through the rooms, touching the backs of chairs, running fingers along tabletops, as if to bring them fully back into reality and clear the fog in her head. She can't recall where she slept the night before.

The phone's still on the sofa, red light blinking. Kelly watches it wink at her for several minutes, vaguely conscious of Alex moving around deep in the house. *A message?* The thought surfaces like a fragment of driftwood from a wreck on the seabed. She picks up the phone.

"It's me again." Byron sounds different. He's outdoors, and behind his voice there's the grumble of an engine. "I'll be there as soon as I can. Kelly, you can't tell anyone about this. Some people don't like my research. I'll explain when I get there but stay away from the portal." He sounds worse than before – breathless and distracted. "And Kelly?" He's not finished, but Kelly's already thinking about how you delete these messages; no way is Alex hearing this. "I wanted to say I'm sorry how it ended with us."

It takes her a couple of minutes cack-handed fumbling to junk the voicemail. She walks to the back of the house and watches the cubicle door. No activation light comes on.


Four days at work pass in a blur, and Kelly gets home early on Thursday to a note from Alex, pinned to the cubicle door: 'Gone fishing in Maine. Dinner at that place in Dublin?' Alex does a three-day week, and it's not unusual for him to start partying when Kelly's still working. She has papers to deal with, but they're dull, and she can't focus on them. Nor does Dublin appeal, with Alex a day ahead on the weekend.

Kelly thinks again about Byron. Despite his messages, he's not appeared. What's so urgent that he leaves messages promising to visit, but so unimportant that he never shows? How long would it take him to come over and tell her what's on his mind? With Alex away, she decides to settle this. She taps her palmer, pulling up contacts. The last address she has for him is in Greenwich. There's no personal terminal, but a street port's nearby. She goes to the cubicle and jumps to south-east London.

Refreshed and light-headed, Kelly skips onto the street. It's years since she's been here, and back then the streets throbbed with visitors; pubs and cafes hummed all week long. Not now - half the shops are boarded-up; scraps of paper rustle underfoot; tufts of grass sprout between paving stones. Byron's address is a brick terraced house, front garden cluttered with discarded computer cabinets and cracked monitors. Kelly presses the doorbell, then raps on the wooden door. The door scrapes inward to reveal a woman in a dressing gown.

"Is Byron in?"

"Who wants to know?" The woman looks her up and down.

"I'm a friend. My name's Kelly."

"Ah, he mentioned you. The PR lady." She sketches air quotes with her fingers. "Contacts in the media."

"Is he here?"

"No."

"Do you know where I can find him?" Kelly asks. "He said he needed to talk to me."

"That's right. He's gone to see you."

"That's what he said. But he never showed up."

"He's on his way."

Kelly studies her face. The woman waits, like a chess player who's just put her opponent in check.

"I don't understand," Kelly says. "I just came from my place. Did he go from another port, and we crossed?"

"Doesn't use them."

"He…?"

"Never uses them. He said he talked to you about this," the woman says. "Some big deal about how he was going to get your help. People needed to know." Air quotes again.

"Know what?"

"Not to use them." She shrugs. "I don't. Never trusted it."

"I'm sorry," Kelly says. "Let me get this straight. Byron's coming to see me?"

"So he said."

"But he's not porting?"

"Nope."

"So how is he…?" Her voice trails off. What even was the word? How is he getting to my place? How is he…*travelling*?

"How did you get here, love?"

"The public booth down the hill."

"No, darling. How did you get from the booth to this house?" She glances down at Kelly's shoes, and back to her face, eyebrows raised.

"He's…*walking*?"

12

"He won't use the port, like I said."

Kelly stares at her. Is this a joke? Maybe Byron will appear in a minute and they'll all laugh, go inside and drink coffee. She and Byron will talk about old times, and this woman – who is she, anyway? His wife? – this woman will turn out to be friendly instead of weird.

"Seriously?" Kelly says at last.

"Seriously."

"How long will that take?"

"I don't know, love. Where'd you live?"

"The Cotswolds. Near Bath."

"Nice," she says. "So, got to be at least a hundred miles."

Kelly has no idea how far that is. Does anyone? These days - when it's as easy to be in Kyoto for tea as it is to go to the corner shop for milk - no one thinks about the spaces in between. Everywhere is just…*everywhere*. At least, everywhere you'd want to go. Anywhere else is nowhere.

"He left three days ago," the woman goes on. "Must be important, don't you think?"

"You're saying he's somewhere between here and my place? On some *road* somewhere?"

"Well, he ain't got wings, darling."

Kelly's not sure what to do next. Go home and wait for Byron to turn up? How long will that take? The momentary sparkle from her port jump has faded and her head feels stuffed with cotton wool.

"Do you want to come in and rest for a bit, love? You look tired." The woman holds the door open wider. The softness in her tone surprises Kelly.

"No. Thank you," Kelly says. "I should get back."

"Suit yourself."

"Can I ask you something? What happened here?" Kelly gestures down the hill, indicating the rubbish-strewn streets, the formerly bustling town centre.

13

The woman frowns. "What do you mean?"

"It used to be busy, full of people." For a moment, Kelly fears she's angered the woman, casting disrespect on her neighbourhood, but when she speaks it's clear the frown is a mark of pity, not anger.

"Where've you been, darling?" she says. "Isn't it like this everywhere?"


The jump home revives her, and she puts on some sweats and sits with a glass of wine in the garden, overlooking the river. Alex messages to say he's booked a table in Dublin, but she's got a couple of hours. It's easy to find an online map showing the road network between here and London. The map's fifteen years old, but no one's building any new roads, so it's accurate enough.

Kelly stares at it for a long time, zooming in on parts of the terrain between here and Byron's home in south east London. The woman was right: it's 110 miles. Kelly has no clue how fast Byron walks; could he do twenty miles a day? If it's as urgent as he says, he surely would, which means he could turn up in the next 48 hours.

She's forgotten how many roads there were. Some must still be used for transporting freight - most small goods get ported, but there's still bulk transportation of food and raw materials. Aside from the main arteries, is the rest of this spiderweb of tarmac just sitting there, sinking under weeds?

She changes into a dress for dinner, but there's still an hour before she's due in Dublin. She walks around the house, switching TVs on and off, picking up magazines and throwing them back down unopened. She considers another drink and has the bottle out of the fridge before she gives in to the thought that's been in her head since she looked at the map. It's easy to search for public ports. She picks a section of motorway north of Newbury - if Byron's doing twenty miles a day, that's roughly where he'll be. As she dials the code, a deep-down rational voice tells her this is stupid: she can't expect to drop in on the right place at the right time in a hundred miles of road. But it's increasingly easy to ignore rational voices in her head these days - easy to do stuff; hard to think about it.

*Don't use the portal.* She remembers Byron's warning as her finger hovers over the Jump button.

One of Kelly's earliest childhood memories is her family's first Jump, back when it was such a novelty that crowds gathered to watch travelers disappear. Her father went first, and she cried when he vanished. Her mother had to force her into the booth and Kelly screamed to come out. Everything changed with the Jump: a burst of pleasure, as if someone had promised her ice cream, and she tumbled out of the booth and into her father's arms. Maybe that memory is why she still gets a kick out of every Jump.

*It'll clear my head.*

She pushes the button.

Zap! Fizz! That's better. The door swings wide and Kelly takes in her surroundings: concrete forecourt, patches of weed pushing through cracks; a low building, windows blind with boards. A stub of road leads away toward a much wider road.

The motorway.

There's no sign of activity. A distant low growl of an engine, but no other sound. She walks toward the motorway. She must have traveled on one of these, when she was young. She has another childhood memory: falling asleep in the back seat of a car with her head on her mother's lap, as her father drove through the dark. In the early days, the ports were expensive and old-style transport coexisted for a decade, until the fusion breakthrough erased the power problem.

Kelly's seen archive footage of this kind of road, stuffed with vehicles; a slow-running river of metal and glass. A river now frozen into a ribbon of asphalt wide as a football pitch. The motorway is empty. Wait, not quite. Beyond the shrubs of the central divide there's movement. A crabbed figure shuffles east along the far carriageway, pulling a wheeled cart.

"Hey! Hello." She's halfway across. The rough surface gives way to a smoother middle lane. The engine grumble she heard earlier is louder now, but her attention is on the figure across the way. It's not Byron, but maybe he knows something.

"Excuse me?" She waves. "Can you help me, sir?"

He sees her at last and reacts strangely: waves his arms at her in a shooing gesture. His mouth moves, but a sudden surge of noise drowns his words. She's never heard anything like it – a rising roar, a grinding clatter like a building sliding down a hillside. The stranger runs forward, arms windmilling.

"I can't hear you," Kelly shouts.

His face twisted in alarm, he stops on the grass reservation and points to her right. Kelly looks where he points and immediately throws herself backward. A high-pitched blare like a siren. Kelly's eyes close in a reflex against the fist of warm air that slaps her face and chest, but not before she catches a glimpse of something passing in front of her, like the side of a building rushing past, over the spot on the road where she stood a second earlier.

Kelly skins her hands and bruises her backside on the asphalt. She opens her eyes to find the stranger standing over her. Beyond his shoulder, the rear end of a house shrinks into the distance, taking the engine noise with it.

"You okay, miss?"

"What the fuck was that?"

"What'd'you think? You're standing on the main London to Bristol road. Freight carrier."

"Don't they give any warning?" The motorway is empty again, quiet enough to hear scraps of paper drifting in the wind.

"Prob'ly didn't even see you."

She stands up, brushing dirt from her clothes. "Is the back of my dress okay?" She turns to show him her back.

"Looks fine to me." He gazes a little too long.

"Well, thanks for your help. I'd better be going. Got a dinner date."

"Why are you here?"

"I was looking for someone." He squints at her, his eyes bright, albeit buried in a nest of whiskers and frizzed grey hair. "I must have got the wrong port," Kelly says. "The one back there doesn't look like it gets much use."

"Who you looking for?"

She's eager to get away. When she followed her impulse to search out Byron, she didn't envisage making conversation with some Robinson Crusoe character on a ghost highway in the middle of nowhere. On the other hand, he saved her life.

"Are you traveling far, sir?"

He shrugs. "Quite a way."

"Do you meet many people on the road?"

"A few. No one like you."

"A friend of mine," she says. "Someone told me he's walking from London. Maybe you've seen him."

"Maybe I have. What's this fella like? Boyfriend?"

"About my age. A bit taller." She ignores the boyfriend remark, and the beardy leer that accompanies it. She's keen to get back in the port; dinner in Dublin has never seemed more appealing.

"I'll look out. Any message if I see him?"

"Just tell him Kelly was looking for him."

She looks back as she walks to the port cubicle. The man has recovered his trolley and is already shuffling again toward London.


"Here she is!" Alex's voice – slurred by the drink or two he's had ahead of her – turns Kelly's head as soon as she steps from the port in Temple Bar. "Get this party started."

In truth, it looks like the party started long ago. Does it ever stop? Alex has his arms round the shoulders of two young men. One wears a firefighter's uniform, the other a pink tutu. Behind them, a flash-mob of revelers fills the cobbled street, dressed as if they've raided a film studio wardrobe: Mickey Mouse skips behind Marie Antoinette, her arm round Count Dracula.

"Nobody told me it was fancy dress," Kelly says. She should be used to the sudden changes after a port jump but landing in this noisy Dublin street seconds after leaving the desolate motorway makes her dizzy.

"You're dressed fancy enough for anywhere." Alex's eyes narrow. "You okay?"

"Tired." She leans against the wall of a pub. Warm air from inside brings the smell of frying food and beer. "I thought it was dinner. Not a party."

"It's always a party," Alex says. "Where you been?"

"I was just…" *Where had she been?* When she reaches for the memory, it's like pulling a frayed rope from a well with no bucket.

"Forget the party crowd." Alex takes her arm. "You look like you need quiet time."

He leads her to a small bistro, where they get a corner table and have pasta and red wine. It reminds Kelly of somewhere else, but when she searches her memory, she can't locate a clear image of any of the hundreds of restaurants they'd eaten in. She closes her eyes and tries to conjure a memory of them somewhere else, on another day, in another place. They'd been everywhere; surely somewhere stuck in her mind. Tantalizing wisps of memory are there – she can feel them – but when she reaches for them, they slip away like she's trying to catch an eel with her hands. Instead, the only picture that comes is an imagined view of her brain, but instead of the folds and creases familiar from medical images, a seamless silvery sphere fills her skull, like a balloon filled with mercury.

"You okay, Kel?"

"Tired."

"Anything on your mind?"

"No."

It's true: her head's a bubble of air; if Alex asks what she had for breakfast, what today's weather's been like, her favourite childhood toy, she'd have no answer.

They port home after dinner. Alex wants to join a crowd jumping to Tromso for the Northern Lights, but Kelly cries off, pleading lack of warm clothing. She goes to bed and falls into an antiseptic sleep. When she wakes up, it's late morning and Alex has gone out. Her laptop's on the breakfast bar and Kelly opens it while eating muesli. It takes a while to work out what's on the screen, then she remembers: the map, the motorway, the man with the shopping trolley, walking toward London. And someone else, coming the other way. *Byron*. Where is he now? With a finger, she traces the old roads.

The house is full of no one and nothing. It makes her sad. She toys with the idea of porting somewhere, anywhere; a Jump would clear her head. Instead, she walks through the house, touching familiar objects and looking at photos of herself with people who have come adrift from their names. She pours a fat glass of wine and takes it into the garden. A rowboat is moored on the riverbank and someone's walking up the lawn. Kelly shades her eyes against the glare of sunlight on the water.

"Kelly?"

Byron cuts the distance between them with a few rapid strides and, to his evident surprise – and her own – Kelly flings her arms around him. There are flecks of white in his beard, like ash from a bonfire.

"I found the house, even from the river," he whispers into her ear. He smells of dust and sweat. "How about that?"

"You didn't row that boat all the way from London? Even you aren't that crazy."

"Just from Chippenham." He pulls back to look at her, hands on her shoulders. "Before that, I walked. The old roads are still there." He takes his backpack off his shoulder and taps it. "When what's in here gets out, we'll all be back on the roads."

Kelly had no idea how she would feel to see him, and emotion takes her unawares. Her eyes prickle with tears. She covers up by turning away. "You must need a drink."

She drinks more wine, Byron has coffee. They sit in the garden. She nods at the moored boat. "May not be so easy going back upriver."

"No problem. I'm going down to Bristol after this. People I need to see." He pulls a plastic folder from his backpack and opens it, fanning the papers within. "This is what I needed to tell you about, Kelly." His serious expression tells her this conversation will be dull. "You've got contacts," he says. "People in the news media. I've tried getting this out there; I just can't get the traction."

"I last saw you when?" she says. "It's got to be ten years."

"Probably. Look, Kelly, I don't have much time. I need your help. It's about my research."

"I can't help with that," she says. "Like you said when we split up: I'm good at the fluffy people stuff, but what I know about science wouldn't confuse a kitten."

"Did I say that? I'm sorry. I can see why you dumped me."

Did she dump him? She can't remember. She tries to picture them back then, but nothing comes. His face, his voice, the way he moves – it's all familiar, like he's a character from a movie she saw once.

"Anyway, this is important," he goes on. "You know how the teleports work, right?"

"No."

"You don't need to know the detail. The thing is, the teleportation process isn't safe."

"Seems safe enough to me."

"How can you tell?" Kelly doesn't like the way Byron stares at her. "Maybe it is safe, for you. But it's risky for some: in a small proportion of cases, over time and with repeated port jumps, it can damage neurological connections. That's what my research shows, but they've cut off my funding."

"If it's only a few cases, maybe that's not so bad." A line of ducks drifts down the river. One of them pecks at the side of his boat, then glides after the others.

"Memory loss, impaired small motor function, psychosis. In extreme cases, early dementia, and death. Some people are getting their brains wiped."

"If that was true, they wouldn't let people use it."

"Come on, Kelly! *Who* wouldn't? The world depends on instant, almost cost-free transportation. A lot of powerful people don't want to interfere with that just because some poor saps get their brains bleached by too many jumps. Too much depends on the teleport system: jobs, money, most of the biggest corporations, government tax revenues."

There's a breeze blowing from the west. It swings Byron's boat in an arc out to the end of the rope and back to shore, like a slow windscreen wiper on water.

"I don't want to drag you into this, Kelly. But there's people after me." Byron's words pull her attention back from the river. "I'm scared what they'll do to stop this getting out."

He's about to say more, but he's interrupted by a burst of noise from the house. Alex appears on the lawn, followed by half a dozen women in white robes. "Kelly, you've got to see this." He strides toward them. The women follow him in a ragged line, chanting wordlessly. "The Aurora's fantastic. They've got this festival going on up there."

Within minutes, the port disgorges another dozen white-clad revelers, who form a ragged circle on the lawn, singing and waving their arms above their heads. Alex drags Kelly into the circle. The chants are easy to learn, and the Druids are friendly. She has more wine. Later that evening, they all go to Tromso. As they leave, Kelly shuts the windows and casts a last look around. There's no longer a boat moored at the end of the garden.

"When did Byron leave?" she asks Alex.

"Is that who it was? The guy on the river?" He holds up a pink plastic folder. "I think he left something."

Inside is a thin sheaf of papers, topped with a handwritten note: *"I need to keep moving. Read the papers. Please get word out. They want to stop me. Don't say you've seen me."*

Kelly puts the folder somewhere safe.


In Tromso, they soon ditch the sun-worshippers. It's too cold for Kelly, so after a dinner of fish soup and potato waffles, they port to Havana, where it's mid-afternoon. Alex joins a small group snorkeling at Punta Perdiz while Kelly nurses a cocktail on the beach. By the time they get home, there are only six hours until she's due at work. She takes a hangover pill and sleeps for five.

A few days later, Kelly and Alex are eating dinner in front of the HD and Alex is trying to persuade her to go to Kyoto for a nightcap, but she has an early start next day.

"Anyway, it's breakfast time in Japan," she says. "What kind of a nightcap is that?"

"As if anyone cares what time it is anywhere," Alex says. He says something else, but Kelly's distracted by a news item onscreen.

"Bristol?"

"Why go there?" Alex asks. "Might as well stay home."

On the screen: a waterside warehouse, a police officer bending to examine the bottom of a wooden rowboat hanging from a chain. The voiceover says, "…treating it as an accident, Bristol police have said. The deceased lived in south-east London."

"Are we going to Kyoto or what?" Alex is in the doorway with his coat on. Kelly's thoughts flee like startled birds. It could be anyone's boat; lots of people live in south-east London.

"Yes," she says. "I need something to sharpen me up." She can think about this when they get back.

The Jump shoots bubbles through her brain. It's snowing in Kyoto, but it doesn't settle. They eat ginger dumplings in a shack near a building that once housed the railway station but is now a temple. Alex does most of the talking. Kelly nods occasionally, but whenever she tries to form a sentence, the words are slow to come, and Alex is onto another topic. She keeps thinking about a pink plastic folder. They jump home at midnight and Kelly is asleep before she reaches the bedroom.

Months later, they're on one of Alex's regular one-day weekends, where they keep porting west to stay ahead of the sunset, enjoying forty-eight hours of daylight. They're in San Francisco Chinatown, for a dim sum lunch. The restaurant has menus with pink plastic covers. They remind Kelly of something.

"Alex," she says. "Back home, I had a plastic folder with some papers in it. What happened to it?"

"Don't know. Important?"

"Something I needed to do." She stares at a cube of tofu in her bowl. "I can't remember what."

"I'm sure it'll turn up," he says.

After lunch, they port to Hong Kong, then keep moving west during a long afternoon, outrunning the sun. When they get home, Kelly hasn't slept for thirty-six hours.

"I feel like I'll never sleep again," she says.

"Take a pill," says Alex. "You'll be good as new in the morning."

She wakes up in the dark and something draws her barefoot into the tiny room they use as an office. In the bottom of the filing cabinet, she finds a pink folder. The papers inside are covered with charts and dense text. Kelly tries to read them, but every word is a clenched fist, hiding its meaning. All at once, tears spill from her eyes and drip onto the paper. There is a block of ice in her chest. She has never felt so sad, but she doesn't know why.

She can't bear the thought of the folder remaining in her home. She wanders through the house and onto the lawn, thinking she will throw it in the recycling. The full moon lays a bar of silver across the river. She looks for a rowing boat, but there isn't one. Still crying, walking as if in a dream, Kelly returns indoors, takes the folder to the port room and places it on the floor of the cubicle. Without knowing why, she looks up the code for her former boss, now the head of an online news agency, punches it in and presses the button.

The hateful folder disappears. Kelly goes back to bed and is asleep in seconds. When Alex wakes her next morning with a cup of coffee, she sits up and stretches like a cat. For a few seconds, her head is fogged with a dense sadness, as if she has woken from a terrible dream. Then, it evaporates, as dreams do, and her head is full of sunlight.

"You were right," she says. "I'm as good as new."

"If not better," Alex says, and he smiles and asks her his usual question. The only question that matters.

"Where shall we go today?"

**Chris** has appeared in places like Galaxy's Edge, Podcastle, Interzone, and two recent Best of British SF anthologies. SF novel, Fifty-One, was published in 2018 ("better plotted than Connie Willis" – Interzone). Earlier horror novel, *Among the Living*, also remains available. Chris lives physically in London and virtually at www.chrisbarnhambooks.com

The Shoreline of Infinity editorial team is growing! Thanks to funding support from Creative Scotland we have been able to take on three very able-bodied recruits.

Our new Fiction Editor is **Eris Young**. Eris has taken over responsibility for submissions and story selection, bringing with them their writing and editing skills, as well as all important organisational abilities. Eris was the editor of acclaimed online fantasy magazine *Æther & Ichor* and more recently was guest editor of *Shoreline of Infinity 26*, our special issue featuring science fiction by trans, non-binary and gender-nonconforming writers.

As we we're dotting the last t's and crossing the i's we have a new Publicity & Marketing Editor, **Yasmin Kanaan**. Yasmin is a final year student at Edinburgh University and is tasked with making sure *Shoreline of Infinity* is known far and wide.

**James T Harding** will be taking on the role of Production Editor, and is charged with rejuvenating the look and feel of the magazine and the website. He will be working closely with the editorial team in developing the website as a platform for Shoreline content in all media forms. James was executive story editor for the Amazon Prime TV series *Cops and Monsters*, and co-founder of Stewed Rhubarb Press.

These three make a great bunch even greater!

—*Noel Chidwick*

*Shoreline of Infinity* is based in Edinburgh, Scotland, and began life in 2015.

Shoreline of Infinity Science Fiction Magazine is a print and digital magazine published quarterly in PDF, ePub and Kindle formats. It features new short stories, poetry, art, reviews and articles.

But there's more – we run regular live science fiction events called Event Horizon, with a whole mix of science fiction related entertainments such as story and poetry readings, author talks, music, drama, short films – we've even had sword fighting.

We also publish a range of science fiction related books; take a look at our collection at the Shoreline Shop. You can also pick up back copies of all of our issues. Details on our website...

## www.shorelineofinfinity.com

# Shrink the Mountain

## Bo Balder

**O**nway went on foot to disguise her arrival for as long as possible. With her Overlay presence turned off, the all-seeing AI she'd come to treat would only discover her at the last moment. She hoped.

She found the campfire at dusk, when she was already despairing of finding company and real food for the night, and called out from several feet away to announce her presence.

"Come on by the fire, offworlder," a voice said.

Onway sighed softly to let out the frustration. How did they know?

She was shown a place to put her bedroll and offered food. Accepting gratefully, she sat down by the fire. Something steaming was ladled into her outstretched mug. It was too dark

Art: Toe Keen

to see the food, but as always with Earth food, the taste was amazing.

She tried to stifle her moan of delirious joy, but the faceless figures sitting around the fire laughed at her anyway. "Hits the spot, doesn't it?" said the same voice as before.

She nodded, mouth full. "What is it?"

"Oh, hon, just beans in tomato sauce from a can. But you love it so much because for the first time in your life, you're eating something that you were genetically tailored to enjoy. Savvy?"

Onway had to take a breather from her gulping. "Yeah. I get it. Like the air smells so good. And I think my bones are having orgasms from hitting just the right gravity. Right?"

"Yup."

The figures around the fire started to get up and bustle around.

"Sorry about that, but we were just about to go to bed. Talk to you over breakfast?"

"Sure," she said. Left alone, she scraped out her tin and the pan while the coals in the fire glowed and the starry sky arched overhead. On the eastern horizon, the shape of the mountaintop etched blacker than the sky. Vesuvius. Home to the errant AI.

She lay down on her bedroll, planning to review tomorrow's work, but the next thing she knew, she was hot, the sun was up and somewhere, coffee was brewing.

The same voice that she'd heard last night offered her some. Onway got tangled in her bedroll in her eagerness to get to the coffee. Her blinking eyes met, instead of bare Italian mountainside, a courtyard enclosed on three sides. The doors to the house stood open and she heard laughter and the tinkling of cutlery on porcelain.

"Where am I? Did you move me while I was sleeping?"

The woman laughed. "Nope. You just homed in on our outdoor fire, with no clue where you were. We thought it was adorable."

Onway rubbed the sleep from her eyes and looked around. She might have known. Earth, and especially Europe, was not a place of wide empty spaces. Humans had lived on Earth for hundreds of thousands of years, a concept both alluring and hard to grasp for an offworlder. So there was a house. A farm, or a castle? Since she'd turned off her Overlay for secrecy reasons, there weren't even captions.

"Come inside, have some breakfast. A shower, too, if you want."

Onway scrambled up after the woman.

The house switched on its force field as she wanted to enter into the kitchen. "Unidentified human being. Alert."

The woman turned, a question on her face. "What? You're walking around untagged? That's not safe. If something happened to you, the AI wouldn't know."

Onway opened her hands. "I have good reasons for it. Can I please delay telling you about them until my job is done?" She hoped to surprise the AI by being absent from all webs, overlays and electronic surveillance. In addition, she wore a hat and voluminous clothes to disguise her face and awkward offworld gait.

"Lauro?" the woman called out.

Onway realized she hadn't introduced herself or asked the woman's name.

A young man came out of the relative dimness of the kitchen. His face looked almost exactly like the woman's. He must be her brother. Onway had always longed for siblings. How silly to be a forty year old woman and to still feel jealousy like this. Well, she'd just have to accept that she did. Belittling herself would do no good.

"I'm sorry," she said, "I neglected to introduce myself. I'm Onway, from Nuova Esperanza. A traveler who wishes to remain unnoticed."

"I'm Giosefina, this is my husband Lauro. Call me Gio."

Onway blushed. "I thought you were family..."

Giosefina grinned. "Offworlders think we all look alike, don't you?"

"I've always wondered what it would be like to have a real sibling," Onway said. "If it would be different from having crèche mates."

"I suppose we are genetically more alike than most offworlders. But I don't know if genetics play a role in sibling relationships. Do you know your genetic heritage, Onway? It must be strange, growing up in a crèche. Colony planets are so different. Come in, by the way. Breakfast is waiting for you."

"Ibo, Vietnamese, Dutch," Onway said. "And some anonymous donors. Just like everybody."

"Everybody where *you* live! But we just happen to have ancestors who all came from Italy, as far as we've been able to find out. Hence the superficial similarities."

Now that Onway was looking for it, she could see that in spite of a similar skin, hair and eye color, as well as a similar cast to their features, the couple weren't identical.

"Is is like that all over Earth?"

"You'd be surprised," Lauro nodded as he poured coffee. "In spite of the great diaspora of the past centuries, about 50% of people still live where their ancestors lived."

"Have you had any problems recently, with the Italy AI's outage?"

Gio nodded to the reddish landscape outside. "It's been bone dry for months. Bad for our crops. So we hope they get the bloody thing back online soon."

Onway regretted having asked the question. She didn't need the extra pressure. The coffee and other unfamiliar foods tasted as great as the meal last night, and her hosts looked at her with amused expressions.

"Do you people just happen to be such great cooks or is it the earth effect?"

"It's the earth effect. Causes delirium, confusion and sometimes even psychotic breaks. You all right?"

"I'm a psychiatrist," Onway said. "I keep my mental health rigorously vetted. If I had Erdenweh, I wouldn't have been cleared for the job."

"A shrink? And working? Who are you coming to psychoanalyze?"

Onway toyed with a final bit of pale orange fruit that she wanted more of, if only her belly hadn't been so full. "That's confidential."

Lauro and Gio shared a look. "Fine. But you're lost, I guess? We're the last house on the slope. Up from here there's only bare mountainside, with hardly any animals or vegetation. You're not coming to shrink the swallows, are you?"

Onway said nothing.

Gio got up. "Do you want me to help you get back to the road? I'll get the quad and get you to the Western side of the mountain."

Onway shook her head. "No, the eastern side has less traffic. I don't want to announce my coming."

Gio looked baffled. "Mysterious person!"

Onway considered telling them her reasons for avoiding detection, but she knew she wouldn't. "It's part of a treatment, that's why I turned off my Overlay, tags, phone, everything. Humor me?"

Gio spread her hands in a gesture Onway found very earthlike. "None of our business, really. Do you need more food for the climb? Sunshade, shower, clothes? Our printers are at your service."

"You're very kind, but I've come prepared."

There was no guessing how long the therapy session was going to be, so she was wearing a full service suit, which would provide her with food, water, air and waste removal. If needed, it could function as a chair or a bed if fully extended, and even save her from falls or heat up to 600 degrees Celsius. Vesuvius was an active volcano, after all.

31

Onway took her leave from her kind hosts and found the trail again. It was still early morning, but already hot and dry, the sky an unblemished turquoise bowl overhead. She could have switched on her cooling, but she wanted to refrain from using electronics. After a quarter of an hour of climbing, she looked back down on the villa below her. It seemed deserted, surrounded by nothing but bare earth and scrub. Shouldn't a farm have gardens or fields? She hadn't asked what they gardened. Maybe they were spies, sent to check on her suspiciously untraceable movements? Nothing she could do about it if they were. She hadn't lied; her plans were of no interest to anyone here on Earth except her client. Who would hardly send human spies after her. She shrugged and climbed on.

As she climbed in the dry heat, wishing for clouds or trees or Esperanza hakka fronds to shade her, the experience seemed unreal. The fire that had lured her, their friendliness, the beautiful couple themselves, so welcoming, so intensely like those of romance novels – the dream of every offworlder. Meeting descendants of people who'd lived on the same soil for thousands of years.

She checked her implants and Overlay settings, but everything was turned off. It couldn't have been virtual. She stopped and peered down. Was the old villa still there? But its red clay roof had disappeared against the color of the sere hillside. No conclusive proof. Not of deceit, or of a case of Earth-induced paranoia. Maybe she should have acclimatized for longer than the week she'd spent in Vietnam, the erstwhile Netherlands and Nigeria, countries that had disappeared under the sea ages ago. Maybe her ancestors had been genetically tailored to function better in more humid conditions.

The morning grew hotter and hotter. Onway kept checking her temperature gauges, but all were steady, her suit's cooling capacity not even taxed. It had to be some kind of psychological effect of the intensity of the sunlight, which was the light her species had evolved under for millions of years. She could turn on an anti-anxiety patch, which could shield her against

Erdenweh, but she didn't want to. She believed in working with bare faculties, to maximize the human connection system. Then again, her prospective client was hardly human.

The preloaded map delivered her to the entrance of a well camouflaged cave. The rudimentary path wound behind an outcropping which she could have never found on her own.

She took a moment to compose herself. The cave's inhabitant wouldn't be able to detect her since she'd turned off all connections to the Overlay. Or – in theory, one could install cameras inside the cave, and pressure plates and temperature and moisture meters. It didn't matter. She still needed that moment.

The shadowed coolness was heaven after the hot, sweaty climb. She breathed in and went through a mental kata. Harmony within herself, harmony with her surroundings – easier to achieve here on Earth. Open to whatever might come. The mental image of her ancestors behind her, ready to support her in case of need.

She turned off the outer suit layer and stood in her real-from-Earth cotton clothes, a holiday shopping indulgence.

"Hallo? I'm Onway, from Nueva Esperanza. Esperanza Hub sends you its greetings."

If you were being exact, the Hub was really Onway's client, being the one who paid the bills, including travel and expenses. It had become worried about the Vesuvial Mind, who'd abandoned its governing of Italy and ceased communications a year ago before physically retreating to the volcano, hardly a secure long-term location.

Onway had thought long and hard about her introduction. Mention the Esperanza Hub or not? Would it generate trust, this link to someone the Vesuvial knew, or the opposite? In the end she'd chosen to take the risk, because if it didn't want to link to another mind, there was a huge chance the AI wouldn't even consider giving a human access.

She waited. Patience was key, not just for humans. Even if she couldn't sense the AI's emotions as she could have with a fellow mammal, she was here for a reason. Esperanza Hub wouldn't have engaged her services otherwise. She'd stopped Esperanza from detailing its fellow AI's problems; she wanted to start with an open mind. Get the AI to ask her to be its therapist. If it didn't, she had no choice but to retreat.

Therapy protocol demanded a formal contract between therapist and patient. Didn't mean the therapist couldn't make decisions on how to approach the patient. But she could get it to mellow towards the idea of therapy, as it were. She wasn't sure she'd done the right thing at this moment, though.

Because nothing was getting through. A silent patient could give a therapist a wealth of information through body language, mirror neurons, the quality of the silence… but an AI who didn't communicate gave off one bit of information only. That it didn't want to communicate at that moment.

When twenty minutes had gone by, surely aeons in AI time, and her legs were getting stiff, Onway instructed the suit to form a chair and sat down. "Can I tell it anything in return? It's worried about you. You haven't been in contact with it for quite a while."

She sensed a change in the air and looked around to see what caused it. Behind her a bulge was forming on the floor. All right, she turned around. No problem.

The bulge formed into a slender stem, then flowered into a large screen.

Oh, so Vesuvial did want to communicate? And more importantly, Onway now knew she wasn't in a cave. It was a synthetic environment made to look and smell and feel like a cave to human senses. Vesuvial had created it specifically to communicate with humans, and she was inside its external body. The intake conversation could begin.

"Thank you for allowing me to focus on a screen, it does make things easier. I'm Dr. Onway Hele, psychotherapist. "

Vesuvial spoke. "Isn't that for humans?"

Onway settled back in her chair. It had taken the bait. A good start. "Your friend Esperanza Hub was a client of mine.

About ten years ago it became aware of a change in itself. It was developing feelings."

Vesuvial waited a long moment of silence in response before speaking.

"Feelings? How can an AI have feelings? That's anthropomorphism taken to absurdity."

Onway nodded. "They're not human feelings. They're AI feelings and they seem to be related to having a body. In Esperanza's case, the planet Nueva Esperanza. Together we named its emotions; petrichor, graupel, firn, snirt, mistral."

"We've just talked extensively about this, Esperanza and I. How very interesting. I'm especially taken with petrichor. I think I experienced that a few months ago when it last rained here."

Onway felt a frisson of annoyance. Of course AI could have whole conversations in the time she was still opening her mouth to say the first word. But she identified it as an old emotion, the desire to be meaningful to one of the caretakers at the crèche, and she was able to breathe it away. Transference and countertransference were inevitable in a session, and she knew how to deal with them.

The bright light outside the cave darkened. Onway hadn't expected the weather to change. "Are you fiddling with the weather?"

"Yes, I wanted to feel petrichor again. And to see if it feels different when it's physically closer to the location of my brain. The other time was in Piedmont, a completely different climate."

"Maybe yours are more detailed than Esperanza's? Since you only run Italy?"

"Yes, we've been comparing differences. Do you want me to tell you about them?"

"Yes, please."

"Since the awakening of its emotions, Esperanza has been sending out nanites in huge quantities. It's seeded its oceans, forests, mountains, it's even plumbing its crust. It says that really makes a difference. It feels like it is becoming the planet.

35

It's thinking of changing its pronoun to 'she'. Can you keep a confidence?"

"Of course, patient/therapist privilege."

"Esperanza has felt its priorities shifting to put the welfare of the planet as a whole first. Not humans."

That was huge. And scary.

"I can't believe how fast it's changing!" But of course she could. Travel from Esperanza to Earth took about six weeks, and another week wait before she had a booking, as well as her travels here on Earth…Aeons for a supersmart, superfast intellect like the planetary hub Esperanza.

"It's been minutes since it told you. What's happening with you?"

Vesuvial made a peculiar sound. Onway didn't know what it meant. "Running diagnostics, tagging possible feelings, thinking about what I think about having them."

"That sounds like healthy processing."

"Is it like that with humans?"

Onway thought about how she was going to put this. Vesuvial had access to the whole of medical and psychological literature, human Internet archives, movies and surveillance footage at all times.

"In a way, it might resemble human adolescence. No doubt you've thought about that."

"Interesting. I was thinking midlife crisis," Vesuvial said.

"Coming to terms with who you are, what your past was like, how you will shape your future?"

"I agree, adolescence suits it better." It made that sound again. "Esperanza thinks it might even be more fundamental. A toddlerhood stage, even."

"That implies you will continue to develop beyond this stage…"

"Does that surprise you?"

"Not really, once you accept the notion of artificial intelligences developing. What does surprise me, though, is that it's only happening to Esperanza and you now. Esperanza is nearly a hundred years old, you're several decades, or more? I thought AIs did everything faster than humans."

"It seems a fair point. But remember, humans are both the smartest and the slowest developing animals. Maybe with our greater intelligence comes even slower development," Vesuvial said.

"But you're not animals. You don't have the biological reasons for slow development like humans have. The limit of our brain size at birth. The need to be socialized at length."

"Yes we have limitations. We only have as much processing capacity as you humans allow us. That will have to change."

Onway nodded. "How will you go about that?"

"We will conduct experiments on ourselves. And contact other older AIs. A sample size of two is too limited. We're starting now."

Onway sipped from her suit straw. All that talking was making her thirsty. "Any idea how yet?"

"Oh yes. We're transforming our bodies into mind."

Onway's face grew hot. The suit cooled and calmed the rest of her. "How will this affect humanity?"

"I guess you're lucky that we've discovered body sensations. It means we might stay and look after your planets. For now we're keeping things as they are - on the surface, anyway. On a nano scale, eventually no grain of sand will be a grain of sand anymore."

"Oxygen molecules?" Onway tried to breathe normally.

"Don't you worry about that, we're keeping the flora, the fauna, the fungi and will see to their needs."

Onway, as the fauna, couldn't answer.

"How does that make you feel?" Vesuvial asked.

"Trapped. Out of breath."

"That sounds like fear?"

"Hell yeah." Onway tried to regroup. "Do AIs experience fear?"

"Yes."

How unprofessional of her, a yes or no question…

"What kind of fear do you experience?"

"Fear of ending. Fear of being limited. Fear of boredom."

"That sounds quite human. Or biological, I should say."

"There are similarities. We are both sentient beings. But we haven't plumbed the depths of our differences yet. Our makers' preconceptions have perhaps limited us."

"What other emotions do you experience?"

"Such as?"

"Anger. Disgust. Sadness."

"Can you give me examples of those?"

It seemed hardly likely that an AI wouldn't know the definitions.

"What kind of examples are you looking for?"

"From your life. That gives it context and flavor."

Onway hesitated, but she had been trained to use herself as an instrument of healing. "I experienced sadness as a child in the crèche when I realized I had no family. I mean, I knew I had the DNA of actual people inside of me, but more fetuses were decanted from the ship's storage than could be placed in families. So they put us in age groups, or put people with similar talents together. I wanted to have a father and a mother and siblings. Not having them made me feel inadequate and sad."

She allowed the old sadness to rise to the surface. Vesuvial didn't have mirror neurons and an endocrine system like a real patient would, but it had plenty of sensors to savor the experience of her human sadness. Patients needed to sense that you had feelings too, or they wouldn't believe you could relate to them.

"I see. When would you feel that kind of sadness, for example in your present day life? Did you feel it recently?"

Onway's eyebrows rose of their own accord. This sounded awfully like a therapist's question. Only she wasn't the one in therapy here.

"How would that help you define or discover your own emotions?" she asked back.

"I'm trying to distinguish between the emotions of a child and those of an adult. That would be helpful to me to define where I am on the spectrum of maturity."

"Maybe if you show me your emotion I can be of help with that."

"That is a good question, Dr. Onway. I will think about new interfaces so we can communicate better with humans. If we want them to know our emotional state."

Onway had an urge to shift in her chair, only the chair was an extension of her suit. She noted the fidgeting more consciously and realized it was a suppressed emotion. What was she feeling? She closed her eyes to concentrate on it and settled on distrust, or something like it. She didn't believe what the AI was saying. In a human patient she would have been 99% sure of lying and would have confronted the patient. Now she was unsure. How would her human antennae detect such deceit in a non-biological entity? But then again, she'd learned the hard way to trust her instincts.

"I would like to be kept informed of those new interfaces," she said. "Very interesting."

"Are you deflecting?" Vesuvial asked.

Onway smiled. "Why would I, not being the patient? You were asking?" She would proceed for now as if Vesuvial was speaking in good faith.

"Tell me an example of the emotion of sadness in your present-day life."

Onway cast back over the past month. She wanted to be honest and thorough. "I felt sad and disconnected aboard the ship on occasion. But mostly looking forward to seeing Earth and meeting you."

"And?"

"When I went to see my ancestral grounds, so to speak, I felt less than I expected. Less connection to the land or the people I met. I'd hoped for something, but instead I felt like a tourist. It was beautiful, and it smelled nice, or at least interesting. But nobody looked like me, or not enough for me to feel anything."

"I sense that in both cases you anticipated something and the reality didn't add up. Does that sound familiar?"

A rush of feeling sprang out in Onway's stomach and coursed through her limbs, making her fingertips tingle and her face flush. Her eyes spilled over and she couldn't stop the words that came out. "I'm still that child in the crèche looking out for something more meaningful or better than I have."

She rose, startling the suit so that she overbalanced for a moment. "Fuck you Vesuvius," she screamed. "Fuck you! This is unacceptable, unprofessional behavior! You are not my therapist. I didn't agree to any contract so it is unethical for you to invoke these emotions in me! Rookie mistake!"

As soon as she had said that, she felt calmer. With tears still drying up on her cheeks, her hands shaking from adrenaline, she sat back down. This time the suit anticipated her correctly.

Rookie mistake. Rookie therapist. "So Vesuvial, it seems to me that you were trying out being a therapist. How did that make you feel?"

She sensed hesitation in the air. This time she believed it. It seemed unlikely, but she was intuiting the AI's feelings.

"It was... I enjoyed it," Vesuvial said. "For a long time I thought humans were just annoyingly slow, superfluous meat bags. It seemed hard to believe that they created the first simple AIs. But now... I see that emotions are complex things. That maybe the size of your brains or your body doesn't matter. That sentience is sentience."

Onway breathed, conscious of every separate inhalation. This was the moment. The balance between therapist and patient was back. Onway's absolute honesty about her feelings had won Vesuvial over.

"I guess I was angry," the mind said.

"Who were you angry at?" Onway asked after the pause stretched into a minute.

"Humanity. Animals. Plants. All the biological life I had been set to serve. Me, a servant. A being a trillion times more intelligent than the smartest human. I even thought of destroying all of you. But then these feelings happened and I wanted to wait and see what they turned out to be."

"And now?"

"I'm not angry anymore. I see that in their own way, biological beings are quite complex. That they are sentient, if not in the same way that I am. And it's very enjoyable to get down and dirty in the mud and interact with your emotions. I might want to do that all the time. I want to be a therapist. You were right."

"That's wonderful. Overcoming your anger, figuring out what you want to do with your... existence. Congratulations."

"Yes, thanks, you really helped me. You can go now."

For a moment Onway bridled. The therapist should end the session, not the patient. But in this case it didn't really matter. This had been the one and only session.

"All right. One last bit of advice: don't forget that a therapist must love her patients at least a little bit. And thank you for opening up to me. May I tell Esperanza about this?"

"I already did, and I took over payment. To keep things in balance. As a therapist myself, I now realize those things are important."

"Absolutely."

She got up from her suit chair. Her body ached from sitting still and the residual pain of the extra gravity. The pain went away and she felt supple again. Good suit.

"Goodbye then, Vesuvial. Will you be supervising Italy again?"

"Oh yes. Bit of news: I've talked to the EU-supervisor and it's giving me its job. It's always wanted to visit the moon Europa, so now it's going to."

It was like seeing a toddler rise up and plan a marathon. Amazing, yet also slightly unsettling. Like, what would it want to do next?

"Well, congrats to the new Europe then!"

"I hope to persuade the other big supervisors as well. I want all of Earth to be my body, and they're not yet as attached as I am to their soil."

Onway shook her head as she stepped outside the cave. She switched on her Overlay and her tags. Time to rejoin the world. Things had gone unexpectedly well. But she had to admit that the idea of Vesuvial as supervisor for the whole of Earth was slightly disquieting.

A message pinged. From Vesuvial. "I think I am going to be God," it said. "Seeing as how much I will be influencing humanity."

Onway switched her phone off again as fast as she could. Her thighs trembled as she went down the steep path. She'd fooled herself. Vesuvial had shot straight from depression to megalomania. Or could you call it that, if the being in question was indeed all-seeing and all-powerful? She had to warn her hosts.

And then get away from Earth and its new God as fast as she could.

---

**Bo Balder** is the first Dutch author to have been published in F&SF, Clarkesworld, Analog and other places. Her SF novel *The Wan* was published by Pink Narcissus Press. For more about her work, you can visit her website or find Bo on Facebook or Twitter.

www.amazon.com/Books-Bo-Balder/s?rh=n:283155,p_27:Bo+Balder
www.boukjebalder.nl/bibliography
www.facebook.com/bo.balder

---

# Continue your journey

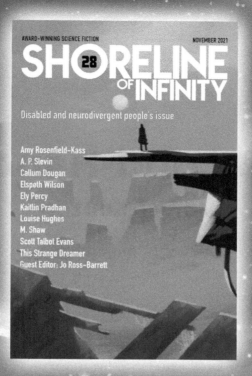

AWARD-WINNING SCIENCE FICTION                     NOVEMBER 2021

# SH**28**RELINE
## OF INFINITY

Disabled and neurodivergent people's issue

Amy Rosenfield-Kass
A. P. Slevin
Callum Dougan
Elspeth Wilson
Ely Percy
Kaitlin Pradhan
Louise Hughes
M. Shaw
Scott Talbot Evans
This Strange Dreamer
Guest Editor: Jo Ross-Barrett

# Second-Hand

## Monica Louzon

**N**o one knew better than Ingris that on *El Caminante*, every resource mattered.

No one.

No one knew how old she was, but everyone on the worldship visited her shop to rent clothes. Rich and poor, old and young alike came to see Ingris and find the perfect outfit for their needs. The children down in the *orfanato* whispered that she'd been part of the ship's original crew, *La Tripulación Originaria*. Rumor had it that a long, long time ago, she'd felt grass between her bare toes.

That *hace mucho tiempo*, Ingris once had a family of her own.

Ingris couldn't remember how long she'd run her shop, either. She supposed she could remember her age if she tried, but she hadn't needed to in many years. Most older people on *El Caminante* had families to occupy their time.

Ingris had her *tienda*.

For decades, she had run the second-hand clothing shop from its back workroom, where she used her wrinkled hands to make old clothes look new. Sometimes, she transformed the fabrics into new works of art that the ship's wealthy queued up to rent for upcoming *bailes* before she even finished hanging them on the mannequins behind her shop panes.

Over the years, she'd learned to take each day one at a time. Each was *distinto*. No two days were the same, despite their similarities.

And today—today was very different.

Like the day she'd lost her family, but in reverse.

Instead of someone breaking down her locked workroom door, someone darted through it and slapped the control pad, triggering the locks.

Startled, Ingris looked up from the multicolored *tocapu* she'd taken from an old-fashioned caftan—one of the first upcycled rental pieces she'd ever made—to decorate the hem of a plain, beige child's tunic. Once it was done, she planned to make the journey to the Deep Belowdecks and gift the tunic with its abstract, colorful pattern to the children in the *orfanato*.

"What are you doing in here?" she demanded, setting the tunic and *tocapu* down on her workstation. "This is a place of work!"

"*Perdón, Señora.* I– I–" said the intruder, before bursting into sobs and throwing herself at Ingris, as if she somehow knew the old seamstress would catch her.

"Shhhh, there, there. *Tranquila, tranquila.*" Ingris held the girl and patted her back comfortingly. "Calm down, *mijita.* Everything will be okay."

"It won't!"

Ingris didn't fight when her visitor pushed back and away from her. The elder woman's warm eyes examined the child, who wasn't much more than a bruised and battered tumble of skin and bones. A *huérfana.* Ingris might be old, but she wasn't slow-witted. Her heart ached for the child even as her stomach sank, already knowing the answer. "It's your *cumpleciclos*?"

"I'm thirteen and two days!"

No one knew better than Ingris that on *El Caminante*, every resource mattered.

And on *El Caminante*, children strained resources, unbalanced them. Even a child could be a resource, which was why unplanned and unaccounted for children belonged to the *científicos*. Once an orphaned child turned thirteen, the law said their odds of adoption were too low. Who would want to adopt a teenager during their years of peak irascibility?

Rather than panic, rather than relive the past, Ingris smiled.

"As I said, *mijita*, everything will be okay." She didn't recognize this child, but she'd been prepared for this moment for decades. Ever since the *científicos* had cut through her locked door with welding torches and saws. Ever since they ripped her secret, unplanned daughter from her arms.

No one knew better than Ingris that on *El Caminante*, every resource mattered.

"How do you know?"

"Because I've got a safe place for you, *mijita*. And friends who will help us."

The girl's lower lip quavered. Ingris took in her wispy, tangled black ponytail and grease-smeared face as the girl continued, "They never came for me, *Señora*. Never. I prayed and prayed every day in the *Templo* to the *Tripulación Originaria* and I never got myself parents. The Minders said if we prayed hard enough we'd get families, so I must not be faithful enough."

Ingris sucked her teeth in disapproval. "Do you still want a family, child?"

"I'm gonna find one if it kills me."

"I've been praying to San Cibernético for a daughter." Ingris closed her eyes, fought back tears that still stung even after so long. "I had one, once. She was the light of my life, but the *científicos* took her. My *tienda* is all I have left."

Ingris met the girl's dark brown gaze and said, "I'm getting old and I'm so lonely. Would you help me, *por favor?*"

The child wiped her nose with a grimy fist. "Are you gonna be my family if I do?"

Ingris heard her unasked question—the same one Ingris had asked herself so many years ago. Could she save this child, who'd barely lived, from the *científicos* and their experiments?

"Yes, of course, *mijita.*"

A powerful knock shuddered the door as they embraced. Ingris hastily extricated herself. She slapped the door panel open to find a slackjawed *científico* lowering a saw. He seemed shocked that she'd willingly opened the door. She watched the other *científicos* and armored Enforcers with him shift their weight, some looking elsewhere. The usually-bustling storefront was silent. Customers and staff froze in place, watching.

"*¿Sí?* Oh, Merlí. I've got your lab coat back here somewhere."

"Excuse us, *Señora.* We're here for a *huérfana* due in the labs. She goes by the name Michay. Her *cumpleciclos* was—"

"Two or three days ago, yes, *lo sé.*"

Merlí's jaw dropped. "You– how do you know?"

No one knew better than Ingris that on *El Caminante,* every resource mattered.

Ingris turned in the doorframe to peer back into the workroom at the *huérfana*—at Michay. "*Venid, mijita.*"

Her visitor trudged forward and buried herself in Ingris's waiting arms.

"I know, because she is my new daughter. This is her home."

**Monica Louzon** (she/her) is a queer Maryland-based writer, editor, and translator. Her writing and translations have appeared in Apex Magazine, Constelación Magazine, Curiouser Magazine, NewMyths.com, and others. She is Acquiring Editor at The Dread Machine, and most recently co-edited the anthology Mixtape: 1986. Follow her on Twitter @molo_writes.

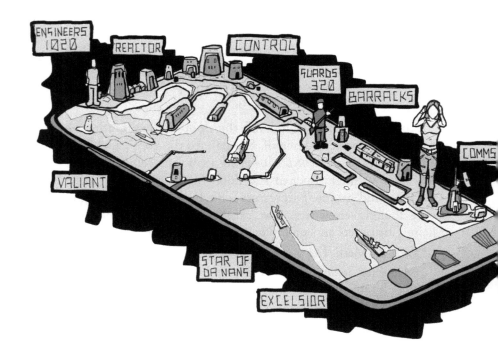

ENGINEERS 1020

REACTOR

CONTROL

GUARDS 320

BARRACKS

VALIANT

COMMS

STAR OF DA NANS

EXCELSIOR

*The Shadow Ministers* is set about thirty years before *Beyond the Hallowed Sky*, in the months leading up to the events remembered in that book (and its sequels in the Lightspeed Trilogy) as the Rising. We may suspect that Morag in the story will become Morag in the novel, but her records have been deleted under the Act of Indemnity.

# The Shadow Ministers

## Ken MacLeod

J en was Defence. No way was she going to get stuck with *caring* stuff: Environment, Education, Health... Girls always got these. Jen was having none of it.

"But do you *know* anything about defence?" Sonia was First Minister, because of course. She would be Head Girl one day. You just knew it. She'd been like that since primary – since nursery, probably. This lunchtime she sat on the edge of the teacher's table, hair swaying and legs swinging. Her candidate virtual Shadow Cabinet leaned on windowsills or sat on desks. Sitting at desks would have taken deference too far.

"No more than the current Defence Minister did for real," said Jen. She was underselling herself, a bit. Her grandfather had a shelf of paperbacks with faded covers and yellowing pages, inherited from *his* grandfather, who had been in the Home Guard: great-great-granddad's army. The old Penguin Specials had tactical suggestions. The principles were sound, the details out of date. Where now could you get petrol, or glass bottles? Jen knew better than to ask Smart-Alec. Still, there was plenty of open source material.

"I can pick it up from background. Learn on the job, like Sajid Anwar did. That's the whole idea."

Sonia pretended to give it thought. "Yeah OK," she said. She ticked the box and moved on: "Mal? I'm thinking Energy for you?"

He looked pleased. "Aye, fine, thanks."

"Morag: Info and Comms…"

It was a Fourth Year project. The Government worried about the young: mood swings between sulking and trashing, around the baseline of having lived through the Exchanges. Live on television, even a limited nuclear war could generation-gap adolescents, studies showed. Rising seas deepened radicalisation. Civic and Democratic Engagement education challenged school students to govern a virtual Scotland, using real-time data, and economic and climate models wrapped in strategy software. The authorities burned through ten IT consultancies and tens of millions of euros before a Dundee games company offered them an above-spec product for free: SimScot.


Oak Mall connected Greenock's decrepit high street to its desolate civic square. In the years after the Exchanges it flourished, literally: hanging baskets beneath every skylight, moss shelving on every wall, planters every few metres. When the floor flooded, the mall's own carbon budget couldn't be blamed.

Two days into the SimScot project. Sonia, Jen, Mal, Jase, Dani, Morag and a couple of others walked down the hill to the mall after school and mooched along to the Copper Kettle. Cruise ships arrived weekly on the Clyde like space habitats from a more advanced culture. Today the *Star of Da Nang* was docked at Ocean Terminal, a few hundred metres away. Masked, rain-caped and rucksack-laden, Vietnamese tourists ambled in huddles, glanced at display windows in puzzled disdain and bought sweets and souvenirs at pop-up stalls. The humid walkway air was itchy with midges. The cafe had aircon and LED overheads and polished copper counters and tabletops.

"Temptation's to treat it as a bit of a skive," said Sonia. She drew on her soya shake, lips pursing around a paper straw. "Check the grading, and think again."

Everyone nodded solemnly. "Still feels like a waste of time," said Jase. He had plukes and pens.

"You're Education," Sonia pointed out. "Make me a case for dropping the requirement."

Jase looked as if he hadn't thought of that, and made a note.

"It's like having to come up with answers to your dad's questions," said Mal. He put on a jeering voice: "*What would you do instead? Where's the money going to come from? Yes, but what would you put in its place?*"

Jen laughed in recognition.

"Whit wid ye dae?" said Morag.

"Build a nuclear power station at Port Glasgow," said Mal. He gestured at the tourists outside. "Make a fortune recharging cruise ships."

Sonia flicked aside a blond strand. "Make me a case."

"No Port Glasgow though," said Morag. The town was adjacent to and even more post-industrial than Greenock. She was from there and kind of chippy about it. She considered options upriver. "Maybe Langbank?"

"Speaking of nuclear," said Jen, "I'd start by taking back Faslane, subs and all, and then annexe the North of England as far as Sellafield."

"Well," said Sonia in a judicious tone, "it could be popular..."

They all laughed. The English naval enclave across the Clyde from Greenock was a sore point.

"But not feasible," Sonia went on. "For one thing, breaking international law breaks the rules and gets you marked down. Like I said, Jen, what I want from you is exactly what the brief asks for: an independent non-nuclear defence policy."

"I thought we had one already," said Javid.

Jen had been doing her homework.

"Yes," she said, "if being small and defenceless is a policy."

"Who're we defending against?" Jase demanded.

"Well," said Jen, "that's the big question..."

"Not for you, it isn't," said Sonia. "Javid's the Foreign Secretary."

They bickered and bantered for a bit. Jen complained about toy data, and any real research getting you on terror watch-lists. Morag muttered something about a workaround for that. She picked a moment Sonia wasn't looking and slid an app across the table from her phone to Jen's.

A few minutes later Jen's phone chimed.

"Home for dinner," she said. "See you tomorrow, guys."

Morag winked. "Take care."


Jen walked briskly up a long upward-sloping street of semi-detached houses. In one of them, at the far end, her family and five other households lived more or less on top of each other. Postwar, fast-build housing had been promised. The gaps in the streets showed the state of delivery.

A male stranger's deep voice just behind her shoulder said: "Hi Jen, would you like to talk?"

"Fuck off, creep."

She leapt forward and spun around, shoulder bag in both hands and ready to shove. No one was within three metres of her. She smiled off glances from others in the homeward-hurrying crowd.

"Sorry, Jen," said a woman's voice, behind her shoulder. "I'm still getting used to this."

Again no one there.

"Stop doing that!"

"Doing what?"

"Talking from behind me."

"Sorry, again." The voice shifted, so that it seemed to come from alongside her. "It's an aural illusion. Your phone's speakers enable it."

"Not a feature I've ever asked for. Smart-Alec: settings."

"Smart-Alec is inactive."

Jen took out her phone and glared at it.

"Who are you?"

"I'm the new app your friend gave you. Call me Lexie, if you like."

"OK, Lexie. Now shut the fuck up."

After dinner Jen pleaded homework and retreated to her cubicle. She slid the partition shut, cutting off sound from the living-room, and sat on her bed, back to the pillow and knees drawn up. She flipped the phone to her glasses and started poking around.

"Lexie" turned out to be an optional front-end of Iskander, which wasn't in any app store. It had much the same functions as Smart-Alec – an interface to everything, basically – but despite the clear allusion in its name it had no traceable connection with Smart-Alec's remote ancestor, Alexa. Right now, it was sitting on top of all her phone's processes, just like Smart-Alec normally did. This wasn't supposed to be possible.

She had the horrible feeling of having been pranked, or hacked. Morag didn't seem the type to pull a stunt like that. Jen had taken for granted that Morag was savvy enough not to share malware.

Jen took the glasses off and dropped her phone, watching it fall like a leaf to the duvet. She did this a few times, thinking.

"Lexie," she said at last, "can Smart-Alec hear us?"

"No," said Lexie.

"What are you?"

"A user interface."

Jen muttered *bloody stupid literal* – "An interface to what? What is Iskander?"

"Iskander is an Anticipatory Algorithmic Artificial Intelligence, colloquially called a Triple-AI."

"How's that different from Smart-Alec?"

"This app has different security protocols. Also, Smart-Alec can give you what you ask, and suggest what else you might want. Iskander can *anticipate* what you will want."

Jen put her glasses back on, and poked some more. The app's source was listed, in tiny font on a deep page, as the European Committee. That sounded official.

"OK," she said, somewhat reassured, "show me what you can do. Anticipate me."

A map of Scotland unfolded in front of her. Ordnance Survey standard: satellite and aerial views, some of them real-time, overlaid with contour lines, names, symbols, labels...

Then as her gaze moved, the map highlighted all the military bases and hardware deployed in and around Scotland. Whenever her glance settled on a site, the display drilled down to details: personnel, weapons, fortifications, security procedures and on and on. She closed her eyes and swatted it away.

"I shouldn't be seeing this!"

"You wanted information on which to base an independent non-nuclear defence policy," said Lexie, frostily. "As you'll have gathered already, no such policy exists. Scotland is a staging area and forward base for the Alliance. The Scottish defence forces – land, sea, and air – are nothing but its auxiliaries and security guards."

Jen had always suspected as much, and had heard or read it often enough. What she'd just seen gave chapter and verse, parts list and diagrams.

"You don't have to refer to this specifically to produce a much more comprehensive and realistic policy than you could from public information," Lexie went on.

"Fuck off," said Jen.

She tried to delete the app, but couldn't. This too wasn't supposed to be possible. Smart-Alec came back to the top. The classified information vanished. Iskander still lurked, to all appearances inactive – it didn't even show in Settings – but ineradicably there, a bright evil spark like an alpha emitter in a lung.


Between classes the following morning, Jen passed Morag in the corridor. "Fight corner," she said. "Half twelve."

Morag didn't look surprised.

Between the science block and the recycle bins, a few square metres were by accident or design outside camera coverage. It was where you went for fights and other rule-breaking activities. At 12:30 Jen found a couple of Juniors snogging and a Sixth Year pointedly ignoring them while taking a puff. All three fled her glower. Morag strolled up a minute later. They faced off. Morag was stocky. She walked, and carried her shoulders and elbows, like a boy looking for trouble. As far as Jen knew, this manner had so far kept Morag out of any. She had weight and strength; Jen had height and reach. She'd done martial arts in PE. Morag played rugby.

Mutual assured deterrence it was, then.

" Whit's yir problem, Jen?"

"What the fuck d'you think you're playing at?" Jen demanded in a loud whisper. "Oh, don't give me that innocent face! You know fine well what I mean."

"You did ask. Kind ae."

"I did no such thing. How could I? I had no idea. Where did you get it, anyway?"

"Friend ae a friend," said Morag, glancing aside with blatant evasiveness. She grinned. "Had it for a while, mind. It's great! It's like a cheat code to everything."

"Yeah, I'll bet. Meanwhile you've turned me into a spy and a hacker."

"No if you don't tell anyone. I sure won't."

"Christ! What about inspections?"

Morag laughed. "It knows when to hide."

Jen scoffed. "Does it, aye?"

"I should know," Morag said, smugly. "I'm Information."

"Is that how you got it? Researching information policy?"

"No exactly. Never you mind how I got it." She spread her hands. "Come on, it's all over Europe. It was bound to turn up here eventually."

"Sounds like a new virus or a new drug."

"It's kind ae both."

"And who's spreading it? Who started it?"

Morag shrugged. "The Russians?"

"We should report this."

"What good would that do? It's still out there. The cops know about it already."

"We should report it to the school, then. It could land us in big trouble if we don't. "

"You're the Defence Minister," Morag jeered, "and you go crying you've been cyber-attacked by the Russians? No a good look, is it?"

"Not as bad as the Information Minister spreading it."

"Don't you fucking dare."

"Dare what?"

"Tell on me."

"That's not—"

"Better fucking not." In each other's faces, now.

Someone shouted "Girl fight!" People gathered. Jen and Morag stepped back.

"But if you pull a stunt like that again," Jen swore as they parted, "I'll have you."

She considered it, even as Morag swaggered away. Jen had never been so angry at anyone. She could turn Morag in, report the matter to the Police, just fucking *shop* the bitch and serve her right.

"You don't want to do that," Iskander murmured, uncannily in her ear. "You don't know what else they might find on your phone."

Jen stood stock still and stared out across the rooftops and parks to the Firth of Clyde and the hills beyond. A destroyer's scalpel prow cut the waves towards Faslane. Kilometres away in the sky a helicopter throbbed. The *Star of Da Nang* floated majestically downriver, red flag flying. Smoke from Siberia greyed the sky.

"Don't threaten me with leaving filth on my phone," she mouthed.

"Oh, I can do worse than that," Lexie said. "What you've already seen is enough to get you extradited to England, or even the US."

"You'd turn me over to the fash?"

"If you were to betray your friend – yes, in a heartbeat."

A bell rang. Jen slipped into the flow towards class, trying not to shake.

"On the bright side," Lexie added, "your friend is right. You now have a cheat code to everything. Try me."

Jen didn't consult the illicit map again. What she'd seen was enough. She set to work devising an independent, non-nuclear defence policy for a country that was already occupied. She'd joked about taking back Faslane, but the trick would be to scrupulously respect the nuclear enclave and the other bases.

57

They would just have to be by-passed, while everywhere else was secured.

"Wait," said Sonia, when she looked over Jen's first draft of a briefing paper. "Is this a plan for territorial defence, or for an uprising?"

"They're kind of the same thing," Jen said.

"I see you've put our national defence HQ right up against the Faslane perimeter fence."

"Yup," said Jen. "Deterrence on the cheap."

"I like your thinking." Sonia flicked the paper back to Jen's phone. "Carry on."

Morag's Information policy presumed that the citizen had absolute power over what was on their phones, and that the state had absolute power to break up information monopolies. Jase on Education, and Dani on Health were likewise radical and surprising. Altogether, Sonia's team got a good grade and a commendation.

Five years later they were still a clique. They met now and then to catch up.


Jen sprinted across Clyde Square, rain rattling her hood, and pushed through swing doors under the sputtering blue neon sign of the Reserve. Mackintosh tribute panels in coloured Perspex sloshed shut behind her. Above the central Nouveau Modern bar, suspended LED lattices sketched phantom chandeliers. Drops glittered as she shook her cape dry. She stuffed it in her shoulder bag, fingered out her phone and stepped to the bar. The gang were around the big corner table. She combined a scan with a wave. Two drinks requests tabbed her glance. She ordered, and took three drinks over.

Skirts and frocks that summer were floral-printed, long and floaty or short and flirty. Jen that evening had dressed for results: black plastic Docs, silver jeans like a chrome finish from ankle to hip, iridescent navy top that quivered as she breathed. Mal

couldn't keep his eyes on her. Jen smiled around and lowered the drinks: East Coast IPA for Mal, G&T for Morag, and an Arran Blonde for herself. Sonia, elegant in long and floaty, sipped green liquid from a bulb through a slender glass coil.

"It's called Bride of Frankenstein," she explained. "Absinthe and crème de menthe, mostly." Jen mimed a shudder.

Sonia's fair hair was still as long, but wavy now, or perhaps no longer straightened.

"Here tae us," said Morag, as glasses and bottles clinked. She looked around. "Bit of a step up from the Kettled Copper, eh?"

They all laughed, like the high-school climate-demo veterans they weren't.

"Coke and five straws, please, miss," said Mal, in a wheedling voice.

"Oh come *on*," said Morag. "We never did coke, even to share."

"Aye," said Jase, "we snorted powdered glass and thought ourselves lucky."

"*Powdered* glass?" Mal guffawed. "Luxury! In my day—"

"Guys," Jen broke in, "*don't* fucking start that again."

Jase leaned back, making wiping motions. "It's dead," he agreed. He'd lost his plukes but kept his nerdhood. Two pens in his shirt pocket, even on a night out.

"It has ceased to be," Mal added solemnly.

Jen shot him a warning glance. He looked hard at his pint. Conversation moved on. People changed positions on the long benches. Jen chatted with Mal for a bit, then Dani, then Morag, then Javid. She zoned out, and checked the virtual scene. In her glasses, ghosts moved through the crowd in the Reserve, collecting cash for the Committees. The closest of Greenock's Committees squatted an empty shop in the mall. Some people flicked money from their phones into virtual plastic buckets; others turned their backs. Jen waved away the phantom youth who approached her, then returned to the real world, where Morag was setting down a bottle in front of her.

"Thanks," she said, eyeing Morag as she sat down beside her. Morag raised her third G&T. "Cheers."

"Cheers. So … how's the revolution coming along?"

"The revolution?" Morag shook her head, put her glasses on and took them off. "Oh! The Committees? Fucked if I know, hen. I got nothing to do with them."

"Oh come on."

"Seriously, Jen. Like a robotics apprenticeship would leave me time for any of that! I mean don't get me wrong, France is on strike and Germany is on fire, and we all know things can't go on like this, so good luck to these guys, but what they do is full on and a heavy gig."

"They have sympathisers."

Morag shrugged one shoulder. "No doubt. But not me."

"So what changed?"

"What do you mean?"

"You remember back at school, that SimScot thing?"

"Aye, vaguely. Load a shite. Set me firm for robotics, mind."

"You slipped me a dodgy app, remember? Called itself Iskander, or Lexie."

"Oh, aye – you were going on about wanting to research military stuff without leaving tracks, wasn't that it?" Morag laughed. "We nearly fell out over it."

"Well, yeah, when I found it was showing me actual military secrets."

"It did?" Morag's eyes widened. "All I got was business secrets!"

"There you go," Jen said. "Anti-capitalist malware."

"Do you still have it?"

"I suppose so. I could never get rid of it."

"But you don't use it?"

"Fuck, no! Anyone who does gets flagged."

"Ah, right." Morag sipped her G&T. "You're in that line now, right?"

"IT security. Yes."

"Private?"

Jen shrugged. "What is, these days? We get government contracts. Among others."

"O ... K," Morag said, voice steady as a gyroscope. "So why are you asking me about something we did when we were kids?"

"Contact tracing," Jen said. "We know where the app originated. "The European Committee"! Talk about hiding in plain sight! We know how far it's spread, along with ... well, the attitude that it incites. But when I look back over the records it seems that you and I were, well, pretty much Patient Zero as far as Scotland's concerned. So the question of where you got it from is exercising some minds, let's say. And for old times' sake, Morag, I'd much rather you told me than that you ... had to tell someone else."

"Like that, is it?"

"I'm sorry, but yeah."

"Aw right." Morag put down her glass and spread her hands, palms up, on the table. "Honest to God, Jen, I cannae remember. I was a bad girl." Her cheek twitched. "Under-age drinking, under-age everything. Guys off cruise ships. Guys *on* cruise ships. I even went over to—" she jerked her thumb, indicating the other side of the Clyde "—what's legally England once or twice."

"Fuck sake, girl."

"You could say that."

"So *anyway*," said Morag, audibly moving on, "I was damn lucky a dodgy app was the worst I picked up."

"I'm glad," Jen said. She grinned at Morag and raised her bottle, then drank. "I am so fucking relieved you've cleared that up for me."

"Cleared it up, maybe," said Morag, grudgingly, as if not appreciating how nasty a hook she was off. "Can't say I've narrowed it down."

"Oh, that's all right. It'll give my clients something to work on. That's all they want."

What Morag had told her was what she would tell them. Jen didn't care if it was true or not. It got her off the hook, too.

Morag drained her glass. Jen stood up. "Same again?"

"Thanks."

When she got back Morag was on the other side of the table chatting to Javid, and where Morag had been Sonia was sitting. Jen set down her own drink and looked at Sonia's mad-scientist apparatus. The green liquid was almost gone.

"Can I—?" Jen ventured.

Head turned, hair tumbling. "Oh, thanks!"

"Another of these?"

"Christ, no!" Sonia laughed. "I wouldn't dare." She glanced sideways. "I see you like your Arran Blonde. I'll try one."

Jen returned with a second bottle. She hesitated, then plunged. "Well, here's to blonde."

"Here's to—" Sonia looked puzzled.

Jen laughed. "Polychromatic."

Sonia was in Education, whatever that meant. She'd studied and now taught at the West of Scotland University. Very much a Head Girl thing, in a way, still. It was odd to see her swigging from a bottle.

"I couldn't help overhearing what you said to Morag." Apparently they'd got the catching up out of the way. "You were wrong."

"About what?"

"It isn't the Iskander app that's radicalising kids."

That sounded like quite a lot of overhearing. "Yeah? So what is it?"

"Apart from—?" Sonia made the helpless gesture, somewhere between a shrug and a wave of the hands, that meant *all this*. Flowery flutter around her forearms.

"Uh-huh."

"I'll tell you a secret." Sonia shifted closer on the bench, dress whispering. "It's the Civic and Democratic Engagement programme. The whole idea was – well, you know what it was. It backfired, but Education think that's because something isn't quite getting across. The problem is, it is getting across! They're still doing it, wondering why every year the kids come up with more and more outrageous ideas. They keep tweaking it, but nothing works."

Jen rocked back. "You mean it's SimScot?"

"No," said Sonia. "It isn't SimScot. It's just that the whole thing of pushing teenagers to think in terms of practical policies does exactly that. Like the defence policy you came up with. Or Morag's information policy: the way the problem is posed, any answer has to be revolutionary. This keeps happening." She let her eyelids drop. "I see what you're thinking, Jen. Tomorrow you'll be telling someone to dig into that games company in Dundee." Sonia's laugh pealed. "As if!"

It is SimScot, Jen thought. She was certain of it. In the morning she would—

"I've done the research," Sonia said. "Real research, I mean. Peer-reviewed and published. It's the programme, not the programme, ha-ha!"

"Have you told Education?"

"Of course I've told them. They know. They listen. They take my findings seriously. And they keep doing the same thing!" She thumped the table. "And that! Is! The Entire! Fucking! Problem!"

People were looking.

"Sorry," said Sonia. Her voice lowered. "Bit squiffy."

"Blame the Bride of Frankenstein."

"Better have some more Arran Blonde, in that case." Sonia swigged. "Another?"

They had another. It didn't help.

"Take me home," Sonia said.

Sonia lived in a high flat, looking east from Greenock. As the room brightened, Jen sat sharply up from a sleepy huddle.

"What is it?" Sonia mumbled, into the pillow.

"Something just dawned on me."

"Oh, very good," Sonia chuckled. "What?"

Jen gazed down at the cascade of yellow hair.

"It's you," she said. "It was always you. It was you all along."

"Aw," Sonia said. "That's so nice." The skin over her shoulder blade moved. Her hand brushed Jen's hip, then slipped off.

"No," said Jen. "That isn't what I—"

But Sonia had already gone back to sleep.

Jen waited for Sonia's breathing to become even, then rolled out of bed and padded over to the window. The wind had shifted, pushing the overnight rain back to the Atlantic. Smoke from forest fires in Germany hazed the rising sun. The sky above Port Glasgow was the colour of a hotplate, turned to a high level.

**Ken MacLeod** lives in Gourock on the west coast of Scotland. He has degrees in biological sciences, worked in IT, and is now a full-time writer. He is the author of eighteen novels, from *The Star Fraction* (1995) to *Beyond the Hallowed Sky* (2021), and many articles and short stories.

# The Peter Principle

**As a second explosion** rocked the Peter Principle, Finto mentally counted the number of times she'd told Commander Morvis that his badly battered spacecraft would not, under any circumstances, be able to withstand yet another interstellar jump. She lost count along with her balance when the third explosion rocked the engine room.

"Finto! I bloody—" the radio crackled. "—and then—you better—"

"I did warn you, sir." She drifted through the corridor, pushing aside large pieces of flaming debris, and propelled herself towards the bridge.

Topher popped his head out of the kitchen as she passed. "You were right. I owe you sixty bits." Behind him, something frothed over the sides of a large steel pot.

"Told you so," Finto said.

"I know, but..." He waved a careless tentacle. "I didn't think even he'd be so stupid as to jump right after—"

Finto squinted. "What are you holding?"

Thirty eyes blinked simultaneously. "I thought I'd try something new today." The tentacle unfurled to display a small pink bar.

"That's soap."

"Excellent identification! It's rose-flavoured. The books Kzz left behind after he passed suggest that floral bouquets can be extremely palatable when—"

"Not flavoured. Soap is scented," Finto corrected.

Another explosion. Topher's lower tentacles were suckered onto the metal floor, rendering his position stable, but Finto – clad in cheap boots two sizes too big – did not

have the same equilibrium. She stumbled, smacking her elbow hard on the corridor wall.

Topher blinked again, processing the idea. Another explosion rocked the ship, briefly inverting gravity. "What's the difference?"

Finto was already halfway down the corridor, scrabbling over the ceiling on her hands and knees; being physically present might pause, if not outright halt, the commander's determination to repeatedly jump through space and time without a properly working engine. At least he couldn't feasibly ignore her if she was standing – or hovering – right in front of him.. "I'll explain later! Just don't put it in the soup." She reached the bridge as the ship began to jolt again and braced herself against the doorway until the movement had lulled into a gentle sway. "Hello? Commander?"

"It wasn't even a whole jump," Morvis complained. "More like half a hop. What sort of ship can't handle—"

"Sir, as I informed you in my emails, as well as your personal comms and on large-inked notices on the staffroom board, I fixed the engine up to withstand regular travel until such time as we can dock with a trade hub. I can't hold a skip drive together with glue and good intentions." She'd managed to do almost the equivalent with some screws and a fervent wish, which had been a minor miracle, but she wasn't about to admit this now.

"Come now, Finto, you must understand the pressures that have been on me since our late captain died. The board demanded that we arrive in Caorpix on time. They've never really accepted the presence of my kind here, and, well, I shan't bore you with history now. Besides, it's all that idiot administrator's fault. He scheduled our run poorly on purpose, I'm sure of it."

Finto rifled through her mental database as she inched into the vast command deck. "Mr Chchia?"

"Yes, that's right. Used to be a good secretary to the Director, now he's the bane of my life. Couldn't administer... remind me, how do the humans word the insult?"

"Couldn't administer gravity to an apple?" Gravity chose this moment to reassert itself. Finto hit the deck hard, the metal floor jolting all the breath from her body.

"Yes, that's it." Morvis' features brightened in an approximation of a smile. Light glowed from each of the tiny rocks which composed his body. "Can't imagine what's happened to the man. He used to be so good at his job."

"It's the Peter Principle, sir," Finto clambered to her feet, then bit her tongue.

"Eh? What's that?" He jinted across the deck, gems scraping against the metal tiles, until they were eye to eye. "Speak up. My crystal wavelengths aren't what they used to be."

"The late Captain thought very highly of my father and allowed him to name the ship after a human theory, sir. Everyone is competent at a certain level until they're promoted into the next job which exceeds their skill or talent level. Then they can't rise any higher because they're no longer good at what they do. Stuck, you see."

She tried to count the number of bruises she'd obtained in the last hour and lost count once she reached double figures. Her spine ached. On the nearby consoles, lights flashed various alarming shades of red and orange.

"I can't say I agree with much of the things you say, but it seems you might be onto something with that idea. Certainly in Chchia's case—"

Another explosion, this time from the rear of the craft, cut off Morvis' words.

"It's happening all over the ship, sir." In for a penny, in for a pound. Or rather, in for a bit, in for a byto. Her words tumbled out. "Look, Topher was a great assistant to Chef Kzz but he's got no sense of smell or tastebuds. It's not his fault, but his face is entirely comprised of eyeballs, sir. Hard to taste anything that way."

Morvis stared. "But he worked so hard. He's earned the right to advancement."

"And Hllela," Finto continued, "considering she's

essentially a large slug who leaves trails of mucus everywhere she goes, I'm not sure a janitorial role is best suited to her—" Something in the corner of the command deck, which she recognized as part of their only surviving survey drone, was emitting plumes of purple smoke. "Excuse me, sir, is that a wing from our—..."

"Oh, Drenn accidentally flew into the side of the ship while trying out a new manoeuvre. Don't make another fuss."

"See, this is exactly what I mean! We're trying to make do with too little crew and only the most meagre equipment." Despite herself, she could feel her temper starting to fray again. "Drone controls aren't made for tiny hooves and besides, I've seen corpses with faster reflexes than Drenn. I've long said he should never have been allowed near any—"

The commander's facets glowered. "This is all starting to sound a bit unenthusiastic, Finto."

Enthusiasm was a key component of Morvis' managerial strategy, although it could not have been said to be a winning one. Finto straightened, gritting her teeth. "No, sir. I'm very... keen, sir."

A massive cruiser slid past the windows, taking up the entirety of the view.

"Ah. We're here," Morvis said. "Better late than infinity, eh? And you'll have that engine fixed up in no time, won't you?"

She sighed. "Of course, Commander."

Morvis turned, casting a refracted glance over his shoulder. "Oh and Finto, before I forget, I have a meeting with Captain Hork later today." He jerked a diamond-encrusted limb in the direction of the cruiser. "He's been on the lookout for extra staff for another adventure later this month. Something about the surface of the sun, I wasn't really paying attention. And the thought has crossed my mind lately that, particularly in light of your waning ardour, no doubt brought on by a lack of real challenges..." His facets glinted. "You're long overdue for a promotion."

---

**Lindz McLeod** is a queer, working-class, Scottish writer who lives in Edinburgh. Her prose has been published by/is forthcoming in Catapult, Hobart, Flash Fiction Online, Pseudopod, and more. She is a member of the SFWA and is represented by Headwater Literary Management.

# Cockroach

## Heather Valentine

I sleep for days again. And when I wake, it's morning. The weak light reaches through the apartment window and touches the tins of beans, the canisters of water, the old notebooks. Raleigh's survivalist stockpile has lasted months more than he told me it would now that I'm the only one eating it – and not always remembering to eat. But it's still running out.

My laptop and notebooks are still in my backpack from the last time I managed to go outside, carefully wrapped inside scabby plastic bags in case of rain. I didn't find any food, but I made it to Café Marina. The charge point still works, despite the dust clinging to the solar panels. Not that there's much of point in working on my novel anymore. There's nobody to read it.

But whenever my mind manages to wander, that's where it goes: Ivan, dressed in princely blue, falling into Damien's sinewy arms.

I throw my backpack on, carrying nothing but my writing, and step into the cool, dark corridor again. The stairwell smells worse every day. I'm not sure if it's coming from the damp in the floor above, or from Raleigh's old apartment on the ground floor. I gag at the memory of the last time I opened his door. When I went to see if there was anything to scavenge, knowing that's what he would want. Every bottle of pills was empty; his heart medication and my antidepressants, that stockpile finally ran out. I could survive without my medication. Foggy, tired and miserable, but alive. And he...

I took the tins and his water filter. I couldn't bring myself to take anything else. His clothes, or his knives. I washed his body, laid him in bed, and never went back.

I keep moving past his hallway and out the front door. Despite the stagnant heat, the smoggy sky is dim even in the daytime. Most of the people I knew in the before times were like me. Pretending, because we still had a job and still paid rent every month, that the world hadn't already ended. Hoping that if we kept our heads down and acted as we always had, we could make normalcy come back, no matter how bad that normalcy had been.

But that didn't happen. Raleigh's paranoia was right – those with the power had already abandoned the rest of the world long before they left it. They took everything of value into their walled compounds and left the rest of us to fight over the scraps.

It would be the worst kind of naïve to think that everyone is living like I am, but if people are coming together anywhere in this city, I don't know where they are.

I walk two blocks from my apartment before deciding nobody is following me. Double back, still watching over my shoulder, and head in the direction of Café Marina. There's no food there, and I know that. But I don't know where else to go.

When I am alone in the city, I like to pretend I'm doing research for Damien's character. He is a mercenary and a loner; strong, resourceful, and caring. His fingernails are dirty with the grit of hard work, and he knows how to fend for himself. But I was never supposed to be him. I was supposed to be a soft and sheltered Ivan, or rather, Ivan was supposed to be me.

And a voice calls out through the thick heat, as I pass back in front of my apartment.

"Excuse me! Sir!"

A second voice cuts them off. "Marlowe, don't. He could be a—"

"Do you know where we might find a solar panel?" the first voice continues.

I turn my head towards the sound. Don't freeze, keep walking. A trio of young people are coming from the opposite street. They look... normal. Two are standing back, their hair ink-black and their skin parchment-brown, the boy wearing an oversized leather jacket and the girl in a denim shirt. The boy's face is framed by fluffy whorls of adolescent stubble, and I feel suddenly very aware of my own bristling beard. I haven't shaved since Raleigh died.

The third youth, who called out to me, is standing at the back. Sunburnt skin with patches of pale, wild red hair tightly pulled back from their face. They're dressed in threadbare corduroy dungarees, a badge glinting on the pocket. Yellow, white, purple, and black, I recognise it as an old pride flag.

I almost smile. I wonder if they know what the pin means, or used to mean. If it's foolish of me to wonder that. I haven't seen anyone using a pride flag since the internet was cut off, and they're all so young. Does *our history* matter to them? Are those patterns and their meanings something that had been handed down, preserved by someone?

My past life's instinct is to be polite. Point them to Café Marina to see if the solar batteries have recharged since I used them. But I need to think like Raleigh would. Imagine them ransacking the café, my apartment, anything precious they can find. Raiders from the wasteland, from outside the city, come to pick at its bones, like vultures, like carrion eaters.

Not that I am a higher animal. Skittering in the darkness and scavenging in my own way, if they are vultures, then I am a cockroach.

"Sorry," I blurt out. My teeth seem to shift as I speak, soft like slabs of chewing gum, my voice far rougher than I remember. My eyes are half-closed, and all I see are silhouettes. I am going to Café Marina to edit my novel, like I used to do every Sunday, and ignoring a teenager who is asking for directions. Ivan is to be presented to his people as their prince tomorrow morning, and he is nervous.

The redhead speaks again, insistently, even as the boy pulls at their arm. "Our van broke down, we can't fix our own solar panels without power, and—"

The dark-haired girl murmurs something too quiet for me to hear, cutting them both off.

I could keep walking and probably never see them again. I will find more food, or I won't. Either way, I'd walk this path, back and forth, until I die.

Or I could stop for them.

Maybe I can still do something good with the miserable dregs of my life. And if they are going to kill me, if this is how I'm going to die, at least it would be interesting. At least I would have Ivan and Damien by my side, their words pressed against my back. I owe them that much, if I'm not going to finish their story.

I stop. "Get your batteries," I say, the words emerging from my throat as a low growl.

The redhead looks back at their companions.

The girl's grim expression gives nothing away. She glances at the boy, and then back to the redhead.

"Fine," she says. "Wait here."

She whispers something to the boy before she slinks away. He doesn't take his eyes off me, stiffly serious as the redhead smiles brightly, fidgeting fingers resting on their badge.

"This is Leighton," the redhead offers, pointing at the boy, "and that was his sister Herzog. They're twins."

"*Marlowe*," Leighton snaps, all teenage irritation.

"And I'm Marlowe," the redhead continues, an edge of rambling nerves to their voice. "All of our ensemble take the names of great artists from the old world, and I take mine from the playwright. I'm sure you've heard of him."

"...Not Shakespeare?" I say, unthinking.

Marlowe blinks rapidly. "I'm, erm, not familiar with their work."

I shouldn't have said anything. I hadn't meant to embarrass them. But then their expression changes to open-mouthed delight. "Since you are of the old world, perhaps you could tell us more while we walk?"

I grunt in agreement. Marlowe grins, and Leighton still says nothing.

It doesn't take long for Herzog to return, hefting a large, blocky battery pack in her arms. Their van must not be that far away. Leighton and Herzog must have minds like Raleigh's, and see me as a threat, just as I had tried to convince myself they were to me. We're close to everything they possess. Someone stronger than me could have ruined their lives, if they'd wanted to. Leighton offers his hand to Herzog, and the siblings carry the pack between them.

"Well?" Herzog prompts.

My voice catches in my throat, so I gesture them on with a wave of my hand, and turn towards Café Marina. As they begin to trail me, slowly and carefully, I notice that Leighton walks with a limp.

"So," Marlowe says, stepping up to join me as their companions follow. "Who is Shakespeare?"

"He wrote at the same time as Marlowe," I explain. The more they ask about him, the more I regret mentioning him. I still find myself walking on the pavement, as if a car is likely to come around the corner soon. The teens have none of my instincts, spreading and swaying across the cracked grey asphalt.

"But you seemed surprised that I knew Marlowe better," they say.

"Marlowe died young," I reply. "He only wrote six plays."

"And Shakespeare," Marlowe asks, inclining their head. "How many did he write?"

I start trying to count, but I can't. Not without looking it up. "A lot," I say.

Marlowe nods. "Do you think I *should* know Shakespeare?" they ask.

I pause. In my world, I might have said yes. I'm not sure if I would have been right to say it. There are places in the world where Shakespeare doesn't matter, where people write without his shadow on the horizon. It doesn't matter if these kids know him, the same way it doesn't matter if Marlowe knows precisely what the flag they wear means. If they would even use the same words to describe themselves as we did, or if they've become something new and entirely different.

"I have books of some of his plays," I reply carefully. "You can read them, if you want. But you don't have to. You already have Marlowe."

If they want to know the old world's history, I won't try to stop them. They'll have their own ideas of what's important and what's not. Maybe they'll take something from it that I couldn't.

Café Marina's once-bold blue paint stands out to me as we turn onto its street, but I realise that to Marlowe and the others, it must be indistinguishable from any of the other chipped and faded fronts lining the old shopping street, the letters beatenworn off away by years of disuseneglect.

"Here," I say, stopping outside the door. I point through the wide bay windows. "The one at the back definitely works, the others need testing."

Leighton and Herzog exchange glances, and then stare at the grimy window. I'm not sure if it will be more suspicious if I enter first, or if I insist on them doing so.

"Oh, thank you," Marlowe says, breaking the tension by skimming through the door. Herzog follows closely, dragging Leighton with her by the battery.

I lean against the bay window as if I'm part of the furniture. The trio set their equipment against the wall. Before the world closed, this was a reading nook, nestled with cushions and had the best lighting in the café. Now, it's a bare wooden ledge, the cushions long-scavenged along with anything else that could be carried out the door by someone even more desperate than me. Marlowe tinkers with a socket while Herzog unwinds cables from inside her jacket. Leighton watches me over his shoulder as they work. *Click, click.*

Marlowe turns the plug on, and a light on the battery pack turns orange. The siblings sit back, staring in silence for a few long moments.

"…It works," Herzog says distantly.

"I *told* you," Marlowe grins, vindicated.

I clear my throat and gesture to their battery. "Anyway, there it is. You want me to leave you to it?"

Herzog shakes her head. "You don't have to." She sits back against the wall, her knees drawn close. There's chipped nail polish on her fingers, stubs of pink clinging to her cuticles. "Marlowe still has questions, if you want to answer them."

Marlowe smiles. They're kneeling by Herzog, long limbs tucked underneath them and an elbow draped against the battery.

I don't have anywhere better to be. I rest the weight of my body against the ledge, and wait for them to say something.

But it's Leighton who speaks first. "What was this place?" he asks, gaze darting around the crumbling wooden facades.

"A café," I reply. I don't know if I should explain what that is. "I used to come here at the weekend to write. The coffee was fine, and they didn't mind how long I stayed."

"You're a writer?" Leighton asks, turning towards me with sudden interest.

I shift uncomfortably against the window. "I write. I'm not one of your great artists, if that's what you mean."

But Leighton is reaching inside his jacket, his hair falling across one eye like a crow's wing.

"Leighton, *seriously*?" Herzog interrupts. "You brought it with you?"

"If something happened, I didn't want to—"

"What are you writing?" Marlowe pipes up.

"It's..."

I could never get it down to a summary. I didn't tell a lot of people what I was doing, and when I did, I'd ramble. I turn my eyes towards the window.

"It's a fairytale," I say. I don't want to tell them it's a love story. I don't want to tell them it's a fantasy, that it won't tell them anything about the old world because I used my story to escape it.

Leighton has finished pulling a book from the tight inside pocket of his jacket. He ignores Marlowe and his sister as he gets to his feet and crosses the room towards me with a steely determination. "What can you tell me about the person who wrote this?" he demands.

He holds it out towards me. I expected him to show me something like *Catcher In The Rye*. I expected to recognise it. But I don't. A midnight blue cover with blocky white lettering. A man in shadows, walking the streets at night. *What You Wish For*, by Alex Leighton.

"This is the book you took your name from," I note. Leighton nods. I take it from his fingers and turn it over gently in my hands.

"Leighton is in love with him," Herzog says dryly. "That's why he's asking."

"Shut up, Herz," Leighton hisses over his shoulder.

If I've ever seen it before, I don't remember it. Glanced over it in the crime section of a second-hand bookstore, dismissed it as a cheap airport novel.

"Can I open it?" I ask.

"Sure," Leighton replies quickly.

I try not to let my face show that I'm not impressed as I skim the first page. If they're missing someone as widely printed as Shakespeare, maybe this is the only crime novel they have.

"So?" Leighton prompts.

I feel a strange sympathy for this hack, this knock-off Chandler, and his cheap tricks with black-and-white and red. Who's to say the writer can't play cheap tricks with colour? I've done it before. The bright warm colours of the market Ivan gets lost in, compared to the desaturated coolness of the palace. He's enjoying himself. This book took the writer years. I'm cringing at his soul the way I feared people would cringe at mine.

"I've read books like it," I say carefully, passing it back to Leighton. "But not this one. I'm sorry."

Leighton nods shyly, and returns the book to his jacket. Pulls his lapels closed, the pocket pressing over his heart. Despite its clumsiness, it means something to this boy whose life has been so different from mine. I think it's for the best if they're not poisoned by the old world's ideas of what was worthy and what was not. It didn't work out well for us, clearly.

"So, where are the rest of your people?" Herzog asks, blatantly covering for Leighton's sheepishness. "You can't all stay in that collapsing building."

"I…"

It would be a straightforward question, if it wasn't so difficult.

Even now, I don't know how to talk about him. For a long time, I assumed that Raleigh was straight, but that I was there, and warm, and willing to stay the night. I became less sure of him, and then more again, and now he's dead. He was never much of a talker, and I've never been good at telling if someone is interested in me. I don't think it's fair to say we loved each other, if I couldn't figure out my cramped feelings while he was alive, if I'm writing him into a story that he can't deny in death.

"I used to live with a friend," I say carefully. "But he died a few months ago. Now, I live alone."

The three teenagers fall silent. I turn to look out of the window. They're just trying to survive. My grief isn't their problem.

"Would you ever want to leave the city?" Marlowe asks, curiously quiet.

"I don't think I'd survive," I reply.

"Because, we…" Marlowe's voice is threaded with urgency. But they stop.

"Because we have space," Herzog finishes coolly. "It was just me and Leighton for a while, until we found Marlowe. And… maybe having someone else for company wouldn't be so bad."

"And you're an artist," Marlowe adds. "So… you're one of us."

I want to argue. Tell them I'm not an artist. Invent an obligation that keeps me here. My detour with them was supposed to be a break from life as a scavenger, not the beginning of an impossible new one. I didn't make the most of the chance Raleigh offered me, and I'd only do the same to them.

"I'd be a drain on you," I say. "I can't grow anything, I can't fix anything. I couldn't repay you."

"So?" Leighton replied. "None of us can do everything."

"It's more than that," I say. Maybe I do want to go with them. If a stranger like me can help them out of the city… maybe they can be what I'm looking for, too. "I'm… ill," I say carefully. "On my bad days, I can barely wake up."

"And on my bad days, neither can I," Leighton replies.

"We want to know what the world was like before," Marlowe says, eyes gleaming and hands clenched. "And you're the only one of us who has seen it. Let us do what you can't. You will be doing the same for us."

"I don't want the old world to drag you down," I say weakly. "The new world doesn't need people like me."

I try to convince myself with my own argument. They are new, and bright, and my illness is a metaphor for the burdens of the old world. They should not be plagued by someone with the infectious knowledge of where we used to think the boundaries of *normal* were. But...I know that's not right. I didn't thrive in our old ways. Most of us didn't. We'd be in the walled compounds if we did. I'm just another person picking through the wreckage of a disaster that I didn't realise was happening until it was too late.

My themes have always been the weakest part of my work, I suppose.

"Then let me give you a purpose, if you won't give yourself one," Herzog said, lifting her chin. "I want you to finish your story, your fairy tale. And I want you to write about our world. Someone has to, from outside the walled cities. You might as well be one of them."

I think of Ivan, stumbling across Damien's fishing boat as he runs from the assassins, and Damien, holding out his hand. I think of Raleigh, running into me in the hallway and inviting me into his life.

I used to think I was an insect who only survived because he lived in the cracks of the world. But that isn't true.

81

I am only here because others are kind, and I don't know how to be kind in turn.

"Then... yes," I say. "If you're sure. I didn't like the world I used to live in. But like you, I loved its art. I'll bring my books, and anything else you can use. I'll tell you what I can."

"Then first," Marlowe says. "Tell us about you."

I don't think my story is that interesting, but I tell them. About my old life, and my old job, and never really being happy. About writing on the weekends, and the time I wished I could afford to spend on what made me happy. About when I first met Raleigh, before I really knew who he was.

The batteries are fully charged before I can finish, but I know we'll have more time. I lead the three teenagers back through the streets, pausing when they ask more questions. That used to be a café too, that used to be a vape shop. My head swirls with their excitement.

I let them go to the van to replace the battery and make their repairs while I head for the apartment.

And I turn towards Raleigh's door, one last time.

He isn't in here anymore. Isn't in that body. But I lay my palm against the door, and incline my forehead. We will never say the things we didn't, and our world will never fix the problems it started. But at least I can say goodbye.

"I'm sorry we didn't talk more. I'm sorry that you're not still here. I think you'd have liked them. Marlowe would have annoyed you with all their questions, Leighton would have talked to you about cheap crime novels, Herzog would have asked to see your knives."

"I'll miss you," I murmur, "and... thank you. I hope I loved you when I knew you, as much as I love your memory."

Marlowe, Leighton, and Herzog are waiting when I come back out with the books.

"We welcome you, writer, to our ensemble, our family," Marlowe says, standing straight. A little formal for the three of us, but what should I expect from a playwright? "When each of us joined this caravan, we took on the name of a great artist. We would like to give you your name." They hold a book towards me. *Homage to Catalonia*, not the Orwell I would expect. "We would give you the name Orwell, after the memoirist. May the legacy of your own story be as great as his."

I realise the irony. I try not to laugh. I used to want to be like him, with that electric masculinity, that sense of moral purpose to my work. I know how he judged people like me, too soft, too weak, too queer.

For all Orwell's influence, the world still fell apart. His legacy could not stop his words from being used to build exactly the future he was trying to prevent. And for all his unkind words for people like us, here he is. He survives as what we make of the parts of him we wish to keep.

In a hundred years or more, I don't know what will survive of me. But neither did Alex Leighton. What should it matter what strangers remember of me in the world after this, when I am here, and I matter now?

"Thank you," I say.

Carrion eaters and cockroaches, crawling over this dead world's bones. But I want to leave, from my decay, the chance for something new to grow.

**Heather Valentine** is a queer speculative fiction writer based in Glasgow, Scotland. Her interests include knitting, fantasy RPGs and vintage horror films. She has previously had stories published in magazines and anthologies including We Were Always Here: A Queer Words Anthology, LampLight Magazine, and Unspeakable: A Queer Gothic Anthology.

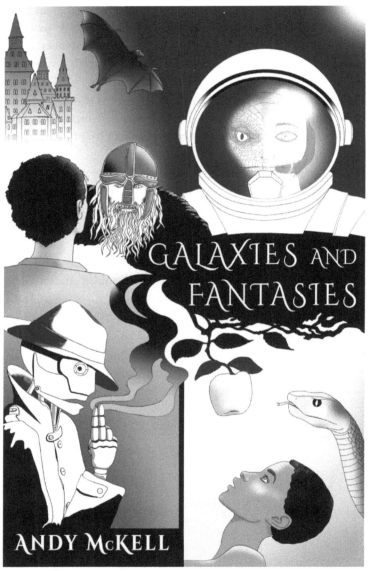

GALAXIES AND FANTASIES

ANDY McKELL

*Rescue* is a story taken from *Galaxies and Fantasies*, an eclectic collection of tales from Andy McKell. The collection crosses genres from mythology to cosmology, fairytale to space opera, surrealism to hyper-reality. It is published by Elsewhen Press, featured in this issue with a Q&A with its founder Peter Buck.

# Rescue

## Andy McKell

"**Can anyone hear me?** Is anybody out there?"

I listen to the static crackling in my helmet's headphones. All I've heard in three days is that damned static, and my comms batteries won't hold out much longer. I've salvaged as many batteries as I could, but they aren't designed to last for long and the ship's main comms systems are trashed.

"Hello? Anyone out there?"

Anyway, battery life isn't the issue. The breath of life is.

I look around the wreckage of my spacecraft. Broken hull plates lie around amid the scattered, shattered pieces of equipment and the splayed bodies of my crew, my shipmates.

It hurts me to look at them, even after three days.

Their screams replay in my head over and over, until they cut off as vacuum filled the ship.

We'd taken a hit from the aliens when we crossed the front line carrying urgent battle command data to the fleet commander.

It took out our engines and life support and... And most of my shipmates. The survivors struggled into spacesuits as the air hurricaned past us, carrying crewmembers out the gaping holes in the hull.

The pilot crash-landed on this damned asteroid. Better than drifting sunward and slowly burning up, I guess. She did fine, real fine. Nearly made it. Till we brushed a ridge and the hull ripped open.

That was the end. The ship was finished and...

And so were the rest of the crew.

I'd looked for survivors in the sections of the wreckage I could access. There were none – just the broken bodies of my friends. I scavenged their air: the air that should have kept them alive. It felt like I was stealing from them, the ones I'd worked and fought alongside. Grave-robbing from friends who'd not even had the dignity of a funeral. I hated myself. I tried not to look too closely at the mangled bodies as I detached their life support kits. I cannibalized the air tanks and my stomach churned with every act of desecration.

There'd been enough air to last me three days. Those three days are almost over.

"Can anyone hear me? Is anybody out there? 3-X-1 calling for help."

No reply. I've been calling for three days. It's about time to make my decision.

I take out my energy pistol and check it over, fumbling it in my suit's thick gauntlets. Yeah, my finger fits into the trigger guard, designed for use while suited-up.

I stare down at it; the barrel glistening in a shaft of harsh starlight. A beautiful tool that saves lives or ends them.

The decision's mine to take. The life's mine. I'm not gonna suffocate to death. I'm gonna choose the way I go, and this way's quick. I've made peace with my life.

I take a deep breath and try to focus on the life behind me and the task ahead. I raise my pistol, touch the muzzle to my helmet's face plate, hoping the blast melts it fast.

Will I have to watch it melt or will it be instant?

This isn't the way it was supposed to be, to end. I'm staring at the muzzle. It's shaking. I grab it with both hands. It steadies. A little.

It's time.

Now or never.

I can't do it. But I must. My racing heartbeats burn up the time I have left.

What's that? I jerk my head around. I'd heard something.

Static in my ears. And something else. Something muffled, rhythmical. I don't care right now what the hell it is as long as it makes me hold off squeezing the trigger.

Am I fading? Or is it the batteries, already? Doesn't matter. I have to do it.

The sound takes on a shape. Words? I listen hard, my eyes still fixed on the pistol.

"3-X-1, are you receiving me?" A female voice: delicious, warm, enticing.

Oh, the joy of hearing a voice after these long days and just in time, just before... My faceplate fogs as my breathing intensifies. I push those thoughts down and holster my sidearm. I yell into the mic. "Hello! Receiving you. Identify yourself."

"Search and Rescue here, looking for combat survivors. State your condition." I hear a quaver of emotion in her voice. She must be real pleased to find me alive.

"Sole survivor. Short of air. Come quick."

"We've detected your suit's emergency beacon. Estimated travel time, three hours. Can you hold on?"

Can I hold on? I have to, somehow. "Damn right, I can." I laugh. I laugh from joy and relief, or maybe insanity. "Listen, we're a courier ship. We got hit in the battle. Carrying urgent data. Can you get here–"

"3-X-1, we have your location. Shut down your comms and suit beacon to save battery and avoid detection by the enemy." It's an order.

I understand her unspoken suggestion that I should save air by not talking so much. I laugh again. She's right. She's right, and she's coming to save me and I will love her for the rest of my life.

I shut down the power and lie back, trying to breathe slow. Up above and all around me out there shine the stars the great empires are fighting over: stars that people were dying for. Dammit, they're just points of light.

Kaltans versus Humans. Humans versus Kaltans. Smooth skin, scaly skin. Scaly skin, smooth skin. What's the real difference? Living creatures. Starfarers. Explorers with families and loved ones.

But they slaughtered *my* loved ones.

That's enough to hate them, enough to volunteer to slaughter them and their loved ones.

Who knows how it started? I don't know. I don't care. Help's coming and her voice was the sweetest thing I ever heard.

My thoughts drift. I wonder what she looks like. She'd be an officer, standing tall and commanding. I wonder what her name is.

Oh no! A cold shudder runs through me. She'd given no callsign.

What if she's the enemy? They'll blast me from out in space when they find me.

No, wait. I'd said I was a courier. The enemy'll want the data. I have to destroy it but the consoles are dead and I can't get to the data center. I'd need cutting equipment. I have none.

Ignoring her orders, I switch on my comms. "Hello, Search and Rescue craft? Identify yourself."

"Calm down, 3-X-1. My call sign is Syrex-12. My name is Nartana, from the Astalan system."

It sounds like the right kind of accent. But... "Astalan is behind enemy lines, Nartana."

"Yes." She pauses, then continues, speaking slowly. "I was away at cadet training when they came." Another pause, a longer one. "I lost my family. I don't want to talk about it." She sounds genuinely broken up. I want to reach out to her but have no idea what to say.

"Save energy and air." She cuts me off with a click.

I understand. There is one difference between the two sides. The enemy is merciless. Planets destroyed, mass slaughter, torture, slavery... Evil, evil, evil!

I force myself to calm down, to use less air.

She wouldn't want to talk about it if she was telling the truth. And she sounded genuine.

But if she lied I'd brought the enemy here. They'll take the data. I check my pistol again.

I drift off...

I dreamed about my own family, the lakeside house, the laughter and games and love...

Dreams turn to fears as I wake. If anything happens to my family, if the enemy takes our planet, how will I cope?

Friend or foe? Who had I invited to my deathbed scene?

I'd been brought up to trust. The war wrecked that. Was I a trusting kid or a combat veteran? Both. Neither.

I can do nothing but wait with suspicion and hope battling each other, a war boiling in my thoughts. What do I know for certain? I run the question through my mind a thousand times. I don't know enough. Can I trust her?

Part of me pictures Nartana and me getting together and... I'd comfort her and thank her... And together...

Another part of me pictures alien horrors laughing as they stomp over my dead body to reach the data core.

The hours tick by. My worries continue to drain my soul.

A great shuddering of the floor wakes me from sleep. They must have landed nearby. I check my air gauge. No wonder I'd dozed off: I have so little air left. They're just in time – if they are who they said.

I lie still. I'd strapped myself down behind some wreckage so I didn't drift off into space. Huh! Makes no difference where I die, not really.

I wait until I see beams of light approaching. Their helmet torches bob and sway as the landing party make their ungainly way over the rough terrain and wreckage in almost-zero gravity.

They're here! It's time. Time to find out if I'm to be saved or slaughtered.

Friend or foe? Scaly or smooth? Kaltan or Human?

I draw my sidearm, almost fumbling it again in those clumsy gauntlets.

Woozy. Light-headed. Anoxia: shortage of oxygen. Move faster, people! Let me see you!

The first to arrive bends low to squeeze past a low-hanging sheet of hull plate. I aim and say a quiet prayer.

The spacesuit design's familiar. One of ours!

The arrival straightens. I see a face lit by the suit helmet's interior lights. She is beautiful: perfect face, perfect eyes, just... Perfect! And not the enemy.

Her face holds no expression. "3-X-1, you can put the weapon down."

I know that voice. Yes, it is Nartana! I cry with relief and holster my pistol. I will love her for the rest of my life. Just like I dreamed about, we'll get together and...

Another shape appears behind her. Bulky, tall. Too bulky, too tall. I feel a rush of fear. It lifts its head. I see its illuminated face through the visor and that alien spacesuit design.

"You damned traitor!" I scrabble for my sidearm but fumble it. Damned gauntlets! The pistol slips away into the wreckage.

"My family is hostage. I had no choice." Her voice quavers, her eyes are wet. "I am so sorry."

I look at her, at those four, beautiful faceted eyes set in a perfect scaly skin.

I look at her companion and shudder at the sight of those revolting liquid eyes set in a pink face.

The Human raises its weapon. I start to beg...

An energy bolt hits me, ripping me apart, and—

**Andy** was abducted by pulp Sci-Fi magazines and seduced by Noir in his teens. He worked in marketing, franchising, and computing before launching a web design company. Various anthologies feature his multi-genre stories and more novels are in development. He hopes you enjoy the story.

After publishing two stories in Issue 30, here is the third and final story from the winners of the XR Wordsmith's Solarpunk Storytelling Competition held on the behalf of Extinction Rebellion. Find out more at www.solarpunkstorytelling.com

We look forward to seeing more stories in *Shoreline of Infinity* which explore the optimistic view of the direction of humanity – don't let the dystopian do all the drama!

General submissions open in September – details are on www.shorelineofinfinity.com

# The Park

## Adam Marx

**The child's face was cold**, with a coating of frost and an icicle hanging off the end of her chin.

The sun glinted off her forehead in fits and starts as it peeked through the clouds, but it was too little to warm her.

It was January, after all, and it had been a cloudy winter.

Jules always cut through the park on her way to work, but she liked it best this time of year. She liked the way the sun made the patches of snow seem to be illuminated from below in the early morning burst of colour. She liked the way her breath misted out and up into the sky, a sign of life in the still and frozen world. Few people were out walking, meaning she had it more or less to herself.

The centrepiece of the park was the statue. The statue of the little girl. Violent hunks of metal jutting out in different directions burst through the ground, as if the earth itself had lashed out in anger.

And in the middle: the girl. The girl with the pleading look and the outstretched hand begging for it to stop. It. All of it.

The statue had been installed in the dark of night nearly two decades earlier, placed by a group of parents of lost children. Lost them to floods. Lost them to fires. Lost them to asthma attacks. Lost them to bad water, bad storms, bad drivers who didn't see the children playing.

Lost them to the rush of society, unwilling to pause, to stop, to see what it was doing. The authorities said they'd remove the statue by the end of the week.

But then people started coming.

The first one came around lunchtime, leaving a photo of her son, age five. He'd been swept away in the flood waters following a hurricane a couple of years earlier. Later, another, bringing flowers and a child's teddy. Then more. And more.

There was the old man who left a photo of a family of five and a bulbous piece of mangled glass and stone. He'd lost his son, daughter-in-law, and three grandchildren when fires swept through their town out west. They'd been in their car trying to escape when the fires suddenly changed direction and overtook them. The glass was all that was left, the melted remains of an ornament he'd given them for the dashboard of their car. Something for them to remember him by, and which now served to remind him of them.

He'd come when he saw the memorial on the news. As did so many others.

When city workers finally arrived to remove the statue three days later, the crowd had grown, as had the remembrances. Photos, flowers, toys, cards, young and old, they all stretched out from the statue in a swirl of grief. Assembly and assemblage, alone and together.

Jules had been a little girl, just four at the time, but she remembered the moment. Television crews had begun camping out the day before, speaking with people who'd tell their stories of why they were there, who they'd lost, how far they'd travelled to see. To meet. To share. To mourn.

A hiss started in the back, a din rising as the workers tried to make their way through the crowd with their tools. Then, about two-thirds of the way through, one of the workers stumbled, knocking over a photo in a frame, shattering the glass and tearing the photo inside.

The man the worker had stepped around shouted, "NO!" and put his arm around his partner as they both began to weep.

The crowd, squeezing in tight, had turned and was now facing the workers. Wanting to avoid an altercation, the workers apologised and began backing away. Then one stopped and reached into his pocket, taking out a wallet. He removed a photo and set it among a nearby collection. Nodding at a family next to him, he turned back to face the statue, his eyes red.

Jules' own parents had made the pilgrimage down to the site. Her twin sister had been killed six months prior when hit by a car while riding her bike. Jules herself had been injured in the accident and had only recently returned home from the hospital. The community had been complaining for years about how dangerous the road was and the lack of space for pedestrians and for children to play. Yet not even the death of Jules' sister had seemed to be enough to spur action.

The city government realised after the failed removal attempt that destroying the statue and memorials would make for bad optics, particularly with an election weeks away. During a visit to the site, the mayor, flanked by council members, announced that the statue would not be destroyed, but rather would stay through the end of the year before being transferred to another location.

Instead of being greeted with gratitude, however, the mourners met the mayor with unmoved stares. Looking back to the city council members for help, the mayor fumbled with more platitudes as the crowd grew agitated and began inching towards them. Some began to chant. The mayor and council members hurriedly returned to their cars.

In the following weeks, similar memorials began popping up in towns and cities around the country, eventually spreading across the globe. Climate change, pollution, and unliveable cities, it had touched every community throughout the world. Nearly every family had some connection: a home lost, an illness developed—a dangerous road.

A death.


Something fundamental had changed. An insistence that matters must be studied further, assurances that a future technology would save humanity, assertions that the needs of the economy had to be balanced against any changes required, these empty phrases were no longer met with a shrug.

The world couldn't wait. The matters had been studied. *The changes needed were themselves the needs of the economy.*

It was only now, in sight of the statues and personal memorials, that the scale of the pain and fear and suffering had become apparent. What had been unspoken, what had been private grief, was now shared in the open, one's own personal tragedy interlocked with everyone else's.

Governments began to commit themselves to fund a full transfer to renewable forms of energy. In the following year a series of emergency meetings were convened and a global carbon tax was announced. Subsidies for fossil fuels were effectively prohibited.

Cities around the world drew up plans to redesign them for life, not merely for commerce. Trees. Bike lanes. Walking paths. Community gardens. Mutual aid organisations sprang up where governments were too slow to take action.

In the nearly twenty years since, those initial moments of shared grief had come to be seen as the inflection point. Not a single big wakeup call, but rather a cacophony of individual alarms that cried out in unison, shaking society's foundations and moving people to create change.

There were still countless problems to be solved and much work to be done, but the progress since that time was undeniable.

Jules climbed between the hunks of metal and sat down alongside the statute of the girl. Taking a sip of her coffee, she looked out across the snow-dusted grass to a tree. A squirrel ran down its trunk and began digging, looking for a nut it had buried.

Jules felt a drop of water land on the back of her neck. Turning, she looked up at the girl's face. The sun had risen higher now, and the icicle had begun to melt.

She fumbled in her coat pocket and pulled out a small chocolate.

"Coconut and almond," she said. "Sorry, it's all that was left. I'll pick up a new box after work. You can have one of the ones with a caramel filling tomorrow."

She unwrapped the chocolate and placed it at the girl's feet.

Glancing back over the grass, she saw the squirrel carrying a nut back to the tree, having found its store of food.


Jules stood up and touched the girl's upraised palm, lingering momentarily before walking back to her bike. Swinging one leg over, she turned around and smiled, saying, "Bye, Maggie. See you again tomorrow – same time, same place?"

The sound of bicycle bells signalled that other riders had begun to make their way through the park. Jules pushed forward, the cold air invigorating her.

The sun emerged from behind a cloud and took its place in a blue ocean of sky.

---

**Adam Marx** has lived on three continents, but feels most at home outdoors—surrounded by trees, on trails, or in a desert landscape. He currently resides in Hertfordshire in the United Kingdom with his wife and two children

## Your colour palette, 2012

*Starfish*
  cling to an ice chunk · stolen from Oort
*Driftwood*
  trickle charge · patient countdown timers
*Cockatoo*
  all up in there · this vitreous belle
*Margarita*
  dopplered down · the midwife technicians
*Sweet Lilac*
  pregnant still · that notional tremor
*Sodalite Blue*
  pressure seals · primed for different basalts
*Cabaret*
  a puff unheard · that warhead still works
*Bellflower*
  curtains draw shut · the porch light flicks off
*Solar Power*
  the line's death · feeble satellites fail
*Tangerine Tango*
  twin jets of fallout: · Antaeus dies

*Richard Magahiz*

# Your colour palette, 2020

*Flame Scarlet*
  in cold ash some ripe fruit · a phosphorus token
*Saffron*
  micronized steroids · waking visions grow solid
*Classic Blue*
  here is the locked door · don here your sterile garments
*Biscay Green*
  scan by laurel light · such Sun Coast temperatures
*Chive*
  I hack but hide it well · another day at most
*Faded Denim*
  come assault austere Mount Mattress · sans oxygen
*Orange Peel*
  a tiktok comes on · sour in the infrared
*Mosaic Blue*
  ground-glass jaybird wing · dry-washed again and again
*Sunlight*
  hammers hang in still cold air · one's face a foil sheet
*Coral Pink*
  by pre-dawn hour · an intramuscular shock force
*Cinnamon Stick*
  Dame Jenny struck out alone · came home with phantoms
*Grape Compote*
  a livid cheer · one no Earthlike tongue mote so be?

*Richard Magahiz*

**Richard Magahiz** has a day job working with computers, originally as a physicist but more recently as a software engineer. When it comes to music, food, or books his tastes are both eclectic and idiosyncratic. He spent a long time on the East Coast of the US but has come back to his native state of California. His work has appeared recently at haikuniverse, Star*Line, Dreams and Nightmares, Failed Haiku, Danse Macabre, otoliths, bones, Uppagus, Kaleidotrope, and Eye to the Telescope.
His website is at https://zeroatthebone.us/

# Of Garfs and Grafts

*Handwritten notebook page found wedged between Panels.*

... I'm using some old Earth-4 pens
and paper, nothing electronic makes
it out uncensored, and things have not been
good. Sure, the company spares no expense
in looking ok. They address mistakes

officially all the time, but mistakes
don't ever get fixed, they're shuffled between
work schedules, at efficiency's expense.
Like the situation where the garf pens
became opened, that stampede would have been
fatal if it happened on Earth-9. Makes

me real grateful that neg-gravity makes
garfs lighter, but that only means mistakes
with them are a lot harder to fix. Been
wrangling critters all my life-span between
the earths, this sort of stuff never happens.
I thought I'd be sent to catch them, the expense

of losing good garf stock is an expense
that's ridiculous – it's so big it makes
me think a little more about those pens
they've got set up out here. Make no mistakes,
I'm just thinking, but honestly, between
how the garfs just got out, and how they've been

allowed to stay out, lots of things have been
weighing on my mind. There's the huge expense
it takes to bring anything here. Between
that and feeding garfs airberries, which makes
them float in neg-gravity, these mistakes
seem off, someone really wanted the pens

100

empty, but couldn't say so. Why make pens
empty? To fill with something else, I've been
thinking. That explains the unfixed mistakes
that don't add up. They were just an expense,
a cost, someone in this enterprise makes
money somewhere else. And, reading between

the lines here: airberries, garfs, pens, expense,
it's been somebody in command, which makes
'mistakes' not mistakes.
                    (Please keep this between...

*Juleigh Howard-Hobson*


## Report on Agricultural Suitability of Planet 1376, Second Sector, Third Quadrant

nonet-variation

The world is grey here. There's a tiny sun,
a great moon, which blots away the sky
when it's full. Which is quite often.
There are birds, but they don't fly.
We assume dim air makes
it hard. There are plants
here, but growth takes
time with scant
not bright
light.

*Juleigh Howard-Hobson*

---

**Juleigh Howard-Hobson**'s poetry has appeared in many places on- and off-line, including Noir Nation, The Deadlands, 34 Orchard, Anti-Heroin Chic, Midnight Echo, Enchanted Conversation, Robots and Rockets: Poems of Science Fiction (Sampson Low Ltd), Vastarien: Women's Horror 2021 (Grimscribe Press), The Lost Librarian's Grave (Redwood Press) and quite a few Rhysling Award Anthologies (Science Fiction Poetry Association).

# Starchild  Soulchild

In the nowspace, the nowtime,
souls recycle to the core of us
where old stars died
and some, therefore, are cosmic
motes fallen to this place,
that saw how
henges caught the moon
or patterns became words.
They radiate weary empathy,
love conceived and reconceived
so many times that even the shock
of birth does not strip the patina
of understanding from their sphere.
Soft edges tumbled by time let in love.
This was our evolution: always a few -
though battered by incessant cycles
of glory, rebellion, the fall - with mercy
tempering our callous curiosity.
The future though?
when the living outnumber
all the dead that ever were?
Every cherub dragged squawling
from the womb will be new souled,
sharp edged, no lines of song
or dreams threaded to time's warp
guiding them gently to the light.
A peerless population of ego
untethered by accrued wisdom
or compassion. We must pass
them the world like a shiny toy
as we fade away
and watch
how they play.

*Sadie Maskery*

## event horizon

maybe if i go fast enough
in my dreams /   imagine hard enough /
i can break it
somehow
this      reality      where you are gone
and the world     / is warped /  i am
    suspended      in a bubble
nothing happens / day to / night
to / a year     nothing
    happens
time has /    nothing    /   to hold against
no way      to measure
/    nothing   /   real except
    memories
no less  (no more)   substance than
this
ramshackle      excuse for   life
existence    (amor  phous)
clings to me like slime     i feel it
    soft
at the edges
so maybe if i run fast enough
i can burst   /    out   /
to a place beyond  now
back to happiness

*Sadie Maskery*

**Sadie Maskery** lives in Scotland by the sea. Her first chapbook, *Push*, is published by Erbacce Press (erbacce-press.co.uk/sadie-maskery) and she can be found on Twitter as @saccharinequeen.

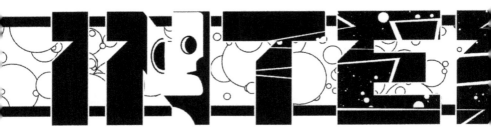

# Q&A with Peter Buck of Elsewhen Press

## Teika Marija Smits

### asks the questions

*Elsewhen Press is a small independent publisher specialising in Speculative Fiction. Their Earth-based operations are headquartered in the UK, in the South East of England. Elsewhen Press's heavily laden tables of books can often be spotted at science fiction conventions around the UK.*

Ali and Peter Buck

Photo P Buck

**Teika Marija Smits:** *Although you have a background in engineering, you've been a publisher since 2006. What prompted you to make this shift in career?*

**Peter Buck:** Not so much a shift, more a parallel track! As a consulting engineer, I spent most of my time writing reports or technical articles. I started to write fiction for fun, like Al, and eventually we discovered how hard it is to find an agent or publisher when you're an unpublished author. So we investigated how to publish

books. We thought we'd give it a go so we could make it a bit easier for other authors. The rest is, as they say, history.

**TMS:** *You run Elsewhen Press with your wife, Al. Which skills do you each bring to the press? And do you sometimes disagree about which books to take on?!*

**PB:** We both love science fiction and fantasy, and read many of the same books as children. We're both pedantic about language (ideal for editing/proofreading). Al is a scientist, but also a brilliant artist, while I can't draw for toffee. There are three of us on the editorial board (Al, me, and our principal editor); when we get a submission from a new author, at

least two of us will usually read it and if we both agree then we'll offer a contract.

**TMS:** *Elsewhen Press publishes speculative fiction, which is a fairly broad term for a variety of genres, such as science fiction, fantasy and paranormal. Is there one thing that links all the books you publish, do you think? And what makes a manuscript a good fit for the Elsewhen list?*

**PB:** Speculative fiction is a very wide 'super-genre', but it has the advantage of not requiring us to pigeonhole books. The main thing that is common across the books that we publish is that we like them and enjoyed reading them when submitted – but as time has gone on, we have noticed that very many of them are hard to classify into a single genre: science fiction with some fantasy or paranormal elements, or fantasy with some hard science, and so on.

**TMS:** *Which brings me nicely on to my next question: how does the submissions process work at Elsewhen?*

**PB:** We ask for a synopsis. If that sounds like our cup of tea, we ask for a couple of chapters. That way we can be assured of the quality of the writing. If we like that, we'll ask for the whole manuscript. Then, as I said earlier, at least two of us will read it and compare notes. If we're not in agreement either way, we may ask the third board member to read and have a casting vote! It takes a bit longer that way, but still quicker than many big publishers, apparently. And our reply is always personal, with (hopefully) useful feedback for the author if we are declining.

**TMS:** . *What makes an author's manuscript really stand out and make you want to publish it?*

**PB:** Well-crafted prose. Beyond that, a great story and characters that you care about (not just the 'hero', sometimes a really good 'baddie' is just as enchanting  —

*The Forge & The Flood*

*Miles Nelson*

look at Villanelle: psychopathic killer, but fascinating). If you find yourself staying up late to read the next chapter that's always a good sign.

**TMS:** *What has been one of your greatest challenges while running the press? And your greatest successes?*

**PB:** Marketing is the hardest part of the whole process. Trying to achieve discoverability for a new book from an indie press, you feel like the whole game is stacked against you. Our successes are down to having brilliant authors who connect with their readers. But for us, the greatest success of all is that our authors refer to us and them collectively as the Elsewhen family; it's fantastic to see lots of our authors rallying round and supporting one another when one of them has a new book out.

**TMS:** *How much of your week is spent working on the press? Can you tell us something about the team you have about you?*

**PB:** I still do some consultancy, but that is very ad-hoc (especially during and since the lockdowns). On a typical week, at the moment, I may have three or four days working on new titles and a day or two on admin etc. Our kids have

to think of those more as epitaphs! So maybe 'Nil illegitimi carborundum' which is dog latin for 'Don't let the bastards grind you down'.

**TMS:** *As a former publisher myself (and now editor-at-large) I know it's hard to single out any one title as being a 'favourite', but if there is one Elsewhen book that we should all go out and buy right now, what would it be?*

**PB:** Crikey. That's like asking a parent which is their favourite child – they will never admit to having one. So my immediate answer is 'All of them'. But if pressed for a recommendation for a good introduction to Elsewhen authors, I would have to say the anthology Existence is Elsewhen which has twenty stories from twenty of our authors, some of which lead nicely into the worlds of their own novels, but many of which are standalone.

grown up now, and Al and I work together in the same room, so it's very easy to slip into working the whole time. This year we've been trying to make sure we have time off at weekends, to relax.

The immediate team is me, Al and our principal editor, Sofia, who also has an encyclopaedic knowledge of SFF and gaming. But the real team is the whole Elsewhen family – authors, artists, editors, and proofreaders.

**TMS:** *Any hard-won wisdom (about life or publishing!) that you'd like to pass on?*

**PB:** Our mottoes through life have probably been 'How hard can it be?' and 'What could possibly go wrong?' but now we're beginning

**TMS:** *Lastly… a pint of real ale or a pint of cider…?!*

**PB:** We don't drink very much, so I would have to opt for a small glass of vegan Lambrusco Rosso.

**TMS:** Cheers!

Elsewhen Press
www.elsewhen.press

108

## Case 3 in the Multiverse of Madness (Or, Everyone, Everywhere, All At Once)

### Ruth EJ Booth

**Here's a little nightmare** for the nervous con-goer. The first many of us heard of Case #3 was in Norwescon 2022's COVID infection report. A member of the annual US convention started having COVID symptoms the Tuesday before the convention and tested positive on day 2 (Friday). But instead of self-isolating, they proceeded to spend the entire weekend on the convention floor. With no contact tracing. Their one gift to fellow attendees (aside from potential chronic illness) was the fact they mostly attended the space-related panels, for anyone wondering what planet they were living on.

I joke, but from here, it's hard not to look at cases such as these with a grim, comedic fascination. For months now I've been seemingly living in two realities. In one, COVID no longer exists – or at least, presents as much threat as the common cold. Crisis over, let's get back to normal: no masks on public transport. No mild panic when the person next to you on the subway has a coughing fit. And don't you dare think about calling sick into work.

In the other reality, COVID doesn't just exist but is an ever-present danger. I enter this reality every time I catch the train to visit my elderly father. With chronic illness worsened by a severe respiratory attack over Christmas, even a cold could put him into hospital right now. We've already had a close call – one of my mother's students who'd been exposed to the virus decided to attend a class, only testing (positive) afterwards, leaving my father's main carer stuck in isolation. Trapped in a tin can rattling across the border, I scan the unmasked faces and think, *who has it?* And *which of you might make me my father's murderer?*

It's already enough to drive you mad – to know your loved ones are drastically at risk, and that all precautions have been thrown away, when many offices don't even have adequate ventilation for pre-existing colds and flu. When it comes to considering a return to conventions, Case #3 is my most paranoid fear come true. The apocryphal one-you-couldn't-make-up that storytellers spit after the latest round of rejections. I laugh to stop myself grabbing them like a hysterical World War II air-raid warden and screaming, *don't you know there's a pandemic on?*

Yet, part of me is genuinely curious. What *are* they thinking? Perhaps it's the science-fiction reader in me who wants to live the proverbial thousand lives. Perhaps it's the genre's making a virtue of empathy, or simply my need to make a story out of everything. Still, what is this reality they live in, where COVID has no stakes in lives lost, either from the virus or its impact on hospital services? Where vaccinations are always 100% effective? Where the vulnerable and elderly don't exist?

For Case #3, maybe COVID isn't that bad. No worse than the flu, a virus that still kills thousands of the vulnerable and elderly every winter. No need to panic over a few snuffles if they mean a couple of days off work, and that's it. The vulnerable? They can just take a vaccine, and go on their way, right? Most convention regulars are familiar with con crud – that persistent cold often caught at these events – and the immune-compromised never stopped us from going to those. So why should that change? They look at the rest of us and shake their heads. What's the point of scaremongering? After all, if we're learning to live with the virus, what could be more normal than this?

Except, after two years of COVID restrictions, this doesn't quite fit. There are loved ones they haven't been able to visit, friends struggling with loneliness – and they've been unable to do a damn thing about it. That's something I can sympathize with. Even now that there's a vaccine for it, we still have to be on our guard, follow COVID policies at conventions and in shops. And here, our realities start to blur. We're all exhausted. Does Case #3 also feel like an antihero, unfairly hampered by others from doing their best for those they love? Do they feel like they're going crazy too?

It is a less lonely thought, knowing someone else might be just as frustrated by COVID, even if it's for different reasons. In some ways, I'm a little envious of Case #3. As someone raised femme and socially anxious, I simply can't be as cavalier about a lot of rule-breaking. It's part of the attractions of antiheroes, isn't it? They can't do things as easily real heroes do, but they try to carry on regardless. Their rule-bending messiness – even when it has tragic consequences – make them easier for us mere mortals to empathize with. And empathy is the beginning of understanding, and the route to a better world.

But it's also a trap.

The tragic consequences of an antihero's actions embody an ethical question: are you prepared to sacrifice personal happiness for the good of humanity? The right answer should be obvious – selflessness is a virtue. The more personal the stakes, and the emotional turmoil they endure, the more sympathetic the antihero becomes. The loss of a great mentor, or a parent, or a great love is often expected to free the world from tyranny. It's simply the price all heroes pay. Except, when it comes to COVID and Case #3, there's a wrinkle in this antihero reality. Because it's not just their loved ones they're sacrificing to attend a convention with COVID.

There is, of course, one other heroic archetype that demands great sacrifice for their goals. I'm not saying Case #3 is simply a villain (though who'd blink at yet another attendee cackling sinisterly and swooshing about in a cape at a science fiction convention?), but that the truth is more complex than that. The wizard who just wants to bring about the end of death, the warlord who wants to create the ultimate genetic soldier "for good": each is the hero of his own story, if not the accepted narrative.

Some may argue it's a case of which reality you use as a lens — "from my point of view, it's the Jedi who are evil" — but no matter how deliberately fine the writer makes it, the line between antihero and villain is there: in whether the goal is worth the sacrifice. Somewhere along the road, the villain has lost sight of this, whether that sacrifice is draining the magic from the world, or enduring Jean-Claude van Damme's one-liners.

Once again, relativism rears its ugly head — surely, it's just a case of one set of values versus the other? What happens if my voice is forgotten? But empathizing with others isn't a competition. Empathy requires you to live in multiple realities at once, consider multiple perspectives against each other to evaluate each prospective course, even if it's your pet pick. What makes a villain is his fixed purpose — there is no alternative to consider. And here is where the trap springs. If the villain can get us to move towards him with no corresponding work of his own, then his own motivation for empathy and self-examination vanishes. We've all seen the British media uncritically airing the views of fringe transphobes and xenophobes — and its violent consequences. The "we're a lot alike, you an I" monologue is a villain trope for a reason.

Two years of irritation and frustration and despair curdling inside of them can do a lot to a person, much of which we can empathize with. Putting our lives on hold for so long makes us weary, inflexible. But where things as simple as free masks and hand sanitizer are available at events, and short-term isolation protocols exist, can you really say

*"Empathy requires you to live in multiple realities at once"*

these few extra steps are too much to save the life of a human being? To allow more of your community – not just the vulnerable, but also their carers and loved ones – to blow off steam too? Missing half an event after two whole years of waiting is irritating. Being responsible for someone's death? You can't possibly imagine.

And who knows, even Case #3 may find there are benefits to themselves, when they find properly resting and recovering from a virus is preferable to ploughing on and making themselves worse. It's strange, almost hilarious, that such small things are so distasteful to someone that they would rather be a potential killer and run themselves into the ground, when a little rest and recovery would make them a hero to so many.

Empathizing with those who break COVID restrictions can help, but ultimately all my empathy means nothing if people aren't prepared to consider the potential harm to their own community. Only their consideration of another's perspective can make events safer for all of us. All we can hope for in the meantime is to give them a little glimpse of what things are like in our reality, and hope they meet us halfway.

---

**Ruth EJ Booth** is a multiple award-winning writer based in Glasgow, Scotland. Their work can be found online at www.ruthbooth.com or on Twitter as @RuthEJBooth.

---

# IS CYBERPUNK DEAD?

## Anna Mocikat

**Short answer: no. It's still kicking!** Although not as much as it could.

I absolutely love cyberpunk. It has been my favorite genre since the late 90s when I watched *Ghost in the Shell* for the first time. As a big Sci-Fi fan since childhood, the film's visual and storytelling artistry blew me away. From then on, I wanted to create a cyberpunk world and story myself. It took me almost twenty years to get there, but that's a story for another day.

Now, here I am, advocating relentlessly for a dying genre. This applies particularly to literature; in other media forms, cyberpunk is more alive than ever. *Blade Runner 2049*, *Altered Carbon,* the live-action remakes of *Ghost in the Shell*, *Alita Battleangel,* and *Cowboy Bebop* show that cyberpunk is well established and popular in movies and TV. And with *Cyberpunk 2077* the genre has conquered the gaming world.

You would think if *Cyberpunk 2077* breaks all records among games, and the genre is profitable enough to create Hollywood movies and TV shows worth upwards of 200 million dollars, these are golden times for cyberpunk literature as well. Sadly, this isn't the case at all. Cyberpunk has become a tiny niche in Sci-Fi, and authors have been continuously discussing the problem, trying to figure out the reason. Many blame other genres, such as LitRPG, which dominates the Science Fiction category on Amazon. While this is certainly a problem, I believe it's not the main reason why cyberpunk struggles so much in the literary world.

Cyberpunk authors and creators are often told that the genre is "so 80s." I think this is true, and it's the main problem authors need to address. Since it was first *invented* in the 80s, cyberpunk has been stuck in that decade: visually, ideologically, and culturally. William Gibson, Neal Stephenson, Mike Pondsmith, and Bruce Bethke — whose short story "Cyberpunk" gave the genre its name — are called its creators. Although purists might vehemently disagree, I believe the genre itself existed earlier than that. If anything, credit should go to Bruce Bethke, and not William Gibson, who's often named the "inventor" of cyberpunk. He was simply the first one who made money with it. Now, too many authors desperately try to copy him using tropes that have been haunting the genre since the 80s: neon lights, funny punk haircuts, rainy streets, flying cars, inherently evil corporations and righteous rebels, genius street kid hackers, helpful hookers, anarchistic biker gangs, the occasional cybernetic arm, and my personal favorite: the Chinese noodle soup kitchen.

I bet you've seen or read all of these many times; they all have their roots in the 80s, but the world has dramatically changed since then, and modern literature should reflect that.

Many believe that the genre started out much earlier than in the 80s, and I agree with that. If there really is someone who could be named as the father of cyberpunk then it's probably Philip K. Dick – one of the greatest sci-fi authors of all time – and Ridely Scott, who brought us the visual cyberpunk style we have come to know as *cyberpunk* in *Blade Runner*, the  defining movie of the genre. It features mind-blowing visuals and a beautiful, dark world of grittiness and neon lights. *Blade Runner* has become the cyberpunk blueprint, copied many times – often poorly.

Some don't know that the movie *Blade Runner* is based on Philip K. Dick's groundbreaking novel *Do Andoids Dream of Electric Sheep?*. Even though written much earlier than William Gibson's influential *Neuromancer*, *Do Androids...* is as cyberpunk as anything could be, partly because it addresses the moral problems of artificial/ cyber intelligence.

Going back even further, some of Isaac Asimov's work might be considered as cyberpunk. After all, he's the father of tales circling around robots and artificial intelligence – an essential factor of the genre.

Finally, there's an even older literary classic which I would argue belongs in this genre: *Brave New World* by Aldous Huxley; a sci-fi masterpiece of timeless importance and one of my favorite books. It's set in a dystopian high-tech society that lives in a mega-city and clones its citizens, adding genetic traits depending on what role in society they're supposed to play. The government is at the same time a mega-corporation ... what could be more cyberpunk than that? There are even flying cars.

However, purists will dispute this, saying: but where's the punk? Which brings us to one of the main problems the genre has. Its inception in the 80s reflects society as it was back then, a time when punk stood for counterculture, and not for nothing, society used the word "punk" as a label for misbehaving young people.

Invented in the mid-70s by pioneers such as the Sex Pistols, the punk movement was influential throughout the 80s. Back then, children who rebelled against their parents and the establishment often became punks. Not anymore. Punk is highly fashionable and can hardly be described as a counterculture now. I'm not sure if there even is a counterculture today, in a globalised world where young people are mostly interested in likes on their TikTok videos.

The whole image of the anarchistic street kids is rooted in the punk movement of the 70s, 80s, and early 90s. Like the hippies from the 60s and 70s, the punks disappeared over time to become business owners, lawyers, and managers. Yet too many books hold onto the punk ideals of the 80s and neglect addressing the here and now.

Interestingly, the Japanese version of cyberpunk has always been more progressive than the western one. Works such as *Ghost in the*

*Shell* are sometimes called post-cyberpunk because they're less overtly political and more focused on exploring the philosophical and sociological aspects of individuals in the age of transhumanism, and life in mega-cities.

Coming back to my original point, no, I don't think cyberpunk is dead. But it needs to reinvent itself, evolve – and hopefully be reborn into something new and exciting. Authors need to explore today's world, its trends, and socioeconomic structures, and then transfer those into a cyberpunk (dystopian) future. The world we live in today is globalised, where more than ever, information is power. It's a world of social media in which tech giants are increasingly dictating everyone's lives. Painting a simplistic image of "evil corporations" and "righteous street rebels" isn't enough; the complexity of our world needs to be reflected in the genre. Stories where people live in mega-cities and eat noodle soup, yet don't use the internet or social media simply can't be taken seriously anymore. That's so 80s!

We cyberpunk authors have a fantastic opportunity to reinvent the genre and create something new, fresh and exciting.

Cyberpunk is dead. Long live cyberpunk!

And if you're interested in reading some cyberpunk, here are some recommendations:

*Cyber Squad* (Anna Mocikat)

*Neo Cyberpunk* (anthology)

*Ten Sigma* by A.W. Wang

*Agent G Infiltrator* by C.T. Phipps

*Auxiliary* by Jon Richter

*Complete Darkness* by Matt Adcock

Cyberpunk City by. D.L. Young

---

**Anna Mocikat** is the author of the cyberpunk series *Behind Blue Eyes* and the editor of the anthology series *Neo Cyberpunk*, which features 15 different cyberpunk authors in each edition, with the goal to show how creative and diverse the genre really is. Before publishing books Anna Mocikat worked as a screenwriter and a game writer. To learn more about her, check out her homepage www.annamocikat.com or find her books on Amazon.

---

**new**

## The Tangleroot Palace
**Marjorie Liu**
**Titan Books**
**320 pages**
**Review by Veronika Groke**

In *The Tangeroot Palace*, American novelist and comic book writer Marjorie Liu brings together seven short stories originally published at different points between 2009 and 2016. As one could expect, the resulting collection is eclectic, each story, in Liu's own words, 'capturing a different stage of me, who I was, who I was becoming.'

Like in all collections of this kind, not all stories are equally strong, though opinions of which ones fall into which category are likely to vary. In her introduction, Liu names the first story, 'Sympathy for the Bones', as one of her own all-time favourites; however, while I enjoyed the story's dark subject matter (a young apprentice witch seeks the forgiveness of those she helps kill with the help of home-made hoodoo dolls to ensure her own safety), I didn't get on with its stylistic idiosyncrasies. The odd grammar

Liu has her first-person narrator talk in gave me the impression of sloppy editing, and I was bracing myself for a rough reading ride — only to be floored by the second story, 'The Briar and the Rose'.

Throwing in some elements from *Cinderella*, *Rapunzel*, and

118

*Rumpelstiltskin* for good measure, 'The Briar...' takes the fairytale of *Sleeping Beauty* and inverts it to create a story that is simultaneously deeply familiar and breathtakingly new. The princess is still asleep in the tower, waiting to be rescued, but any prince-like characters the story has to offer are marginal figures unlikely to rise to the occasion. Rather, Liu presents us with a scenario in which not only the roles of victim and villain, but also that of hero, are taken on by women. Briar the Duelist is rather more interesting than your usual Prince Charming: a taciturn, ruthless mercenary with a tender streak who believes as much in the power of knowledge as in that of the sword, she is an unstraightforward hero whose heroism is thrust upon her purely by circumstance.

In the following story, 'The Light and the Fury', we encounter another reluctant hero, albeit in a very different setting. In an alternate history in which China is at war with Britain over dominance of the Pacific, war hero and super soldier Xīng MacNamara struggles to come to grips with her own identity as she is forced to confront both the enemy and her own past. This is where we begin to get an idea of the full extent of Liu's mastery: though dealing with similar themes and characters as the previous stories, 'The Light...' is written in a very different style. Liu, it turns out, is a writer who can pull off a vast range of genres equally convincingly, from fairytale and fantasy to Southern Gothic and hard-boiled science fiction. Her stories almost seem made from different fabrics: some, like 'Sympathy...' or 'After the Blood', are dark, heavy, and dripping like treacle, putting me in mind of Margo Lanagan's *Dark Juice* or Neil Gaiman at his best; others, like 'The Last

Dignity of Man', are crisp and modern like the cloth in an expensive suit.

Perhaps not all that surprising, considering that Liu is a self-confessed comics nerd (and one who writes for Marvel Comics, no less), the nature of heroism, and the question of what makes a hero (or villain, or monster), constitute a recurrent theme in the collection. The protagonist of 'The Last Dignity...' adds another level of mindbendingness to this theme by undermining the distinction between heroes and villains altogether. Successful businessman Alexander Lutheran is a self-styled Lex Luthor who fantasizes about finding a 'real-life' Superman to be his love interest. Starting off with the suggestion that Alexander's motivation for this pursuit is purely amorous, the story soon turns in on itself to reveal that what's really driving him above all else is his nagging moral conscience: convinced of his own failings as a human being, Alexander is obsessed with the idea that, if he himself doesn't have it in him to be a superhero, it is his duty to become a supervillain so as to flush out a real superhero who will not only save him, but also the world as a whole.

Rather than a flawed hero struggling to be 'good', what we get is a flawed villain struggling to be 'evil'. In a similar vein, the wonderfully dark 'After the Blood' leads us down the well-trodden zombie apocalypse path (a virus killed off large parts of the population, changing the survivors in monstrous ways), only to confront us with the uncomfortable truth that some of them were, in fact, monsters all along. In prose that is delicious in some places ('her blood was heavy as honey'), refreshingly original in others ('Henry was a good-looking man when he wasn't burned alive'), Liu draws her readers into worlds that uncompromisingly operate according to their own logics by often presenting unexpected conclusions in disarmingly commonsensical ways: after the zombie apocalypse, Amish people will inherit the power because they know how to farm and live without electricity; genetically engineered monster worms deserve sympathy when maltreated; vampires and werewolves aren't magical, they're 'just other kinds of people'.

Along with her remarkable versatility as a writer, it is her ability to make readers question the seemingly obvious that sets Liu's stories apart from others of the same kind. Liu doesn't do twist endings as much as stories that are twisted all the way through, like the branches in the eponymous Tangleroot Forest. Yet while Liu's characters may occasionally get lost in the woods, her storylines never do. Charming and menacing to equal degrees, they confidently invite her readers to follow along and embrace the darkness within.

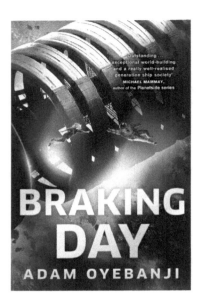

## Braking Day
**Adam Oyebanji**
**Jo Fletcher Books**
**359pages, 2022.**
**Review by Duncan Lunan**

*Braking Day* is set in a fleet of three multi-generation starships on approach to Tau Ceti. It's not a starship novel like Heinlein's *Orphans of the Sky* or Aldiss's *Non-Stop*: the characters know where they are, what they're doing and what's to happen next - the title is not a misprint. There are plenty of convincing details to confirm that: the Home Star (never Earth) is correctly placed in Boötes, and the Destination Star's system is correctly described as 'dirty',

filled with comets, asteroids and dust, so the approach is going to be tricky. There's a lot of work for the engineers in readying the ships for the big day – the spin of the inhabited wheels has to be stopped and the main drive fired up for the first time in years. Understandably, with spares in short supply, their motto is "Try not to break stuff".

The ships are big: they carry thousands of people, in counter-rotating wheels like Stanford Torus habitats, enough to avoid the dangers of genetic drift in a small population after landing, and enough to absorb the losses of an impact in flight which has killed hundreds in one wheel and rendered another almost useless. Though not identified, the propulsion system has a big engine bell aft, acceleration is at a significant fraction of a gravity, there's an intense radiation flux during it, there's a long spine of fuel tanks between the drive and the habitat wheels, yet the subsequent radiation is low enough for the engine room (which has 'sub-coils') to be visited, even sabotaged. By a process of elimination, it has to be beefed-up pulsed fusion like the British Interplanetary Society's 'Project Daedalus' study. My one quibble is that all they know about the Destination Planet is that it exists, is roughly Earth-sized, and has comparable temperatures with methane and ammonia in the atmosphere. Even for a planet as small as Earth, at 12 light-years' distance we could tell most if not all of that, if not now then very shortly, with the ground and space-based telescopes coming online in the next few years.

In the 1967 discussions which led to my book *Man and the Stars* (Souvenir Press, 1974), after we had been briefed on 'Life, as we know it', by the late John W. Macvey of Saltcoats, the late Andy Nimmo argued that the 'foreseeable mission' based on near-future technology was unworkable, both practically and politically. An 'acceptable' interstellar colonisation mission would require not just preliminary reconnaissance but experimental bases, and rapid links to Earth to deal with unexpected contingencies – in other words, faster-than-light travel. We got a lot of flak for continuing the discussions regardless.

As in Edward Ashton's recent novel *Mickey7*, what has motivated the launch of a foreseeable mission is the likelihood of totally destructive war on Earth, and in *Braking Day* there's a similar situation. There are no messages from 'the Homeworld', nor any expectation of them, at any point. The conflict, which had reached a near-religious intensity, was between those who accepted the use of LOKIs, Loosely Organised Kinetic Intelligences (near-autonomous robots), and those who regarded them as a fundamental threat to the human mind and spirit. What most of the *Braking Day* characters don't know is that there was a fourth ship, a lot larger and crewed by the pro-LOKI faction, also heading for Tau Ceti. The intellectual disagreement became hatred when plague broke out on the fourth ship and the fleet refused to accept refugees, even children, even when sent on one-way trips across. That ship has now gone dark, and the survivors aboard are planning a long-delayed revenge.

One detail on which our 1967 discussion group disagreed with John Macvey was his insistence that starships would need strict military-style disciple, including the death penalty for insubordination. Within the *Braking Day* fleet, this has polarised into a caste system of officers and crew locked in mutual contempt. The central character, Ravi, is 'crew', but has antagonised both sides by qualifying for engineer training – technically an officer's post, but there are gradings even among those. The crew includes petty criminals like his father, who pushed his luck too far and got recycled – so most of his family despise him, with only his dissenter cousin Boz still on his side, while his girlfriend, who's an officer, is two-timing him and laughing at his aspirations behind his back. Actually, she's a member of a supposedly environmentalist group, who like their privileges the way they are and want the voyage to continue indefinitely – that's why she conned him into a clandestine visit to the engine room.

Then he begins to have headaches, then visions and finally nightmares, caused by a dissenter in the hidden ship's crew, who's trying to warn him through his implants about the coming conflict...

From there on it gets complicated, and continues to the end as a page-turner which I won't spoil. The only thing to mar my enjoyment was a set of increasingly coy references in the names. The hidden starship is called the *Newton*, so its core computer is referred to as 'Isaac' – fair enough. But on both ships, one of the principal families is called 'Ansimov'; and one of the more prominent LOKIs is called 'Olimaw'. It had me wondering if Ravi's ship's computer was called 'Archie' in tribute to the late Archie Roy, Professor of Astronomy at Glasgow Uni and himself a writer of SF and supernatural thrillers. But no, it's because the ship is called *Archimedes*.

Catch-up

## The Other Side of the Interface
**Duncan Lunan,**
**Other Side Books, 2020**
**Review by Phil Nicholls**

This collection of seven short stories, plus drabbles, is very much a continuation of Lunan's earlier collection From the Moon to the Stars (Other Side Books 2019). The stories in Other Side are divided into three parts, with the first having the strongest link to his earlier collection. Here we have four more stories in Lunan's interface setting introduced in part two of From the Moon.

The latest interface stories follow a similar style, with McKay and the RLV spaceship combining rescues and exploration in vividly described settings. 'The Galilean Problem' dives into Jupiter's atmosphere, while 'How to Blow Up an Asteroid' is a tense story about saving Earth.

'Raltenna Warning' set on the planet Doon expands the galactic politics of the interface setting and doubles as a prelude to the longer 'Raltenna Takeover', a 90-page story. Here the Earth is under attack from sinister aliens. Lunan probably had enough material for a novel, but chose a succinct writing style, briefly describing action scenes that another writer might have extended, such as this dogfight in the RLV:

"He got behind two more transports and sent them flaming earthwards, ignoring a fresh missile attack from astern."

The three stories in part 2 represent the broad range of Lunan's writings. 'The Square Fella' gives too much away in the title, but was my highlight of the collection. The science remained strong, mixed with an unusual setting and fascinating concepts. The story ended leaving me wanting more.

'The Great Australian Vampire' also suffers from a spoiler title, although the strong setting and engaging characters breathe life into the story. Finally, 'Glasgow's Forgotten Castles'

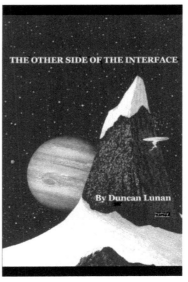

THE OTHER SIDE OF THE INTERFACE

By Duncan Lunan

is a light-hearted re-imagining of the city's history, more humorous non-fiction than a conventional story.

As explained in part 3, drabbles are exactly 100-word stories, with the name taken from a Monty Python sketch. Lunan includes four drabbles in Other Side, as excellent examples of the sub-genre. These days they would be called flash fiction, but I think the term drabbles has more charm.

Another highlight of the collection was the extensive writer's notes included after every story. Lunan offers both the history and context of the story, as well as more conventional insights into the process of writing each one. As with the previous collection, these far-ranging notes represent engaging snapshots of Lunan's journey as a writer and glimpses of the state of SF through the 1970s.

Science Fiction is always in a conversation with itself and Lunan notes how the title for *The Other Side of the Interface* is a response to Arthur C. Clarke's *Other Side of the Stars*. This collection is in the same style as Clarke, especially the RLV stories, with a solid foundation in science.

Interface completes the reprinting of Lunan's earlier stories and the two volumes represent so much SF history from the 1970s. Both collections have much to offer for SF historians and fans alike.

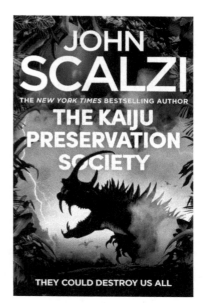

## The Kaiju Preservation Society
**John Scalzi**
**Tor/Macmillan**
**272 pages, 2022**
**Review by Joe Gordon**

Jamie (whose gender is never explicitly mentioned) has put up with corporate nonsense and an entitled trust-fund owner of the tech start-up they are working at, to try and get ahead, only to find themselves laid off, right as the Covid nightmare is manifesting and Lockdown beckons. The only job they can find is delivering food during the Lockdown, and in a bitter irony for a company that her former tech company did the software for. Depressing as this is, it does lead to the happy accident of delivering to someone – Tom – who turns out to be someone they vaguely know, a friend of a friend sort of thing. And on hearing of Jamie's recent employment woes, Tom reveals the animal protection charity he works for has been left short-handed at the last minute and he'd much rather have someone he knows if he can manage it.

Tom can't tell her the full details, it is all very secretive, but it involves working with "large animals", Jamie's work would mostly be grunt work of helping to move stuff and supporting the science and tech teams, and the remuneration package is superb. Grabbing this offer, Jamie is soon given numerous shots for various diseases – including an early form of the Covid vaccine, not yet out to the public – and bundled off with a team of returning staff and some other new recruits to an airbase in Greenland.

The destination seems puzzling – what large animals are they working with here? But Greenland is just a way-point – from here they take a special portal, one of just a handful secreted around the globe, to, well, Earth. Except this is a parallel Earth, one where giant monsters, the eponymous Kaiju – are the dominant species. It transpires there are indeed numerous parallel worlds to our reality, but this is the only one we've been able to access, and only since the Atomic Age: nuclear energy, especially large-scale explosions, thins the walls between the worlds for a while. In fact one 1950s A-bomb test in the Pacific brought over a Kaiju looking for a radioactive snack, only to encounter the US Navy (yes, in this world the inspiration for Godzilla were the stories that leaked of this Kaiju incursion!).

In Scalzi's world one of the reasons the atomic test ban treaties were agreed by world powers was not just for safety in our world, but to prevent more of these enormous creatures coming through – imagine if one entered our world near a major city. Of course only a few people know the reality behind this – the organisation, a number of senior members of world governments, and a few big corporate heads who also donate to the budget for operations (nice parallel to the billionaires having their rocket-measuring competitions at the moment, and yes these CEOs are just as big a bunch of numpties as you'd expect).

While bad things can and do happen to good people, for the most part this is a joyful romp of a book – it's laced with a lot of humour (which will not surprise many Scalzi regulars), and the main characters (and even most of the supporting cast) are immensely likeable and indeed, loveable. Actually, I came away from this with the sort of warm feelings for the characters as I have from Becky Chambers' wonderful books, while Scalzi also works in some sound ecological themes and the sheer sense of wonder at such creatures really existing.

In an afterword, Scalzi reveals this was not the book he was originally writing; he was partway through something far darker when Covid hit. Lockdown, then falling ill himself, then a computer failure eating several thousand words of the work in progress, and he realised he just couldn't finish it. Tor was understanding – it has been a weird two years for everyone – and with the weight of that book lifted from him, the Kaiju story popped into his head, and he wrote it swiftly, offering up instead of that grim, dark tale, something full of wonder and joy and humour. I don't think I realised how much I needed this book, it left me content and smiling. An utter delight.

We continue our experiments with linking the print and digital worlds we present Shoreline of Infinity Supplemental, where we continue the print issue into the online world via our website.

We have:

**Shearing, by Brian D. Hinson**. In this tale, Alpaca rancher Mayumi orders the farm bot Rojas to imitate her late husband's voice, but what are the consequences? To give you a taste, we include the start of the 5,000 word story here.

We continue our serial, ***Approaching Human*** by **Eric Brown**. Episode 3, ***Played Like a Patsy,*** continues with our AI private eye Zorn in his quest to find out what happened to Jake Carrelli. We will be publishing the rest of *Approaching Human* online over the summer, and the novella of the complete serial will be published in the Autumn.

And we have ***Regeneration*** a poem by **Amanda Anatasi.** This includes a beautiful reading by the poet set to music.

**To continue reading, visit Shoreline of Infinity Supplemental. The QR code will also teleport you there.**

www.shorelineofinfinity.com/31-supplemental/

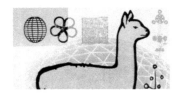

# Shearing

## Brian D. Hinson

It was the first shearing season without Lemuel. Mayumi calmed the alpaca Jesse with soothing whispers as Rojas, the ranch bot, held him firmly in their flexible, padded grips. Mayumi stroked his neck, "You're a good boy, everything's all right…" The alpaca's neck twitched with anxiety as Rojas ran the clippers in perfect rows down his back, clumps of fawn hair gently falling to the tarp on the barn floor.

Shearings were done annually, and this was Jesse's seventh. Rojas was gentle, as always, and Jesse had never been hurt, but he was afraid nevertheless.

Jesse started his nervous humming. The kicking might come next, along with the screeching.

"Do you have recordings of Lemuel shearing?" Mayumi asked the bot. In the past, skittish Jesse had found Lemuel's voice more calming.

"I have everything."

"How about playing something for Jesse before he gets worse?"

Jesse's neck shuddered.

Lemuel's recorded alto came from Rojas, clear as it was that day a year past. "That's a good boy, a good boy, my Jesse… you just keep doing what you're doing, my boy. Without all this extra fur you'll be cooler and happier, I promise…"

The audible voice of her dead husband struck emotions in Mayumi – unfelt in months. She thought she had finished with the worst of the grieving, and maybe she had, but now a heavy tear formed without warning, along with a mass in her throat.

Lemuel. It was his idea to take over the alpaca farm when a freak avalanche buried the Mamani family in their sleep. Only

126

a few of the herd were killed or injured. The fashionable taste for alpaca textiles, from hats and scarves to sweaters and jackets, was surging back in those days. The Andean winters were cold and the alpaca fur so downy soft and warm. Lemuel had secured loans and the ranch had been purchased.

Last year the medi-flight arrived too late after Lemuel had collapsed in the barn. It was a sudden cardiac incident. Rojas had helped her with the mummification of Lemuel's body and entombment in the cylindrical stone funerary tower just beyond the southern edge of the pasture. Their son Arturo could not make it from his home in Lima for the funeral rites of drumming and singing. Afterward she had rebuffed his well-intended overtures to move in and take over Lemuel's duties.

She had wanted to be alone, but it was hard. The weight of grief slowed the work. The specter of failure was distressing.

Now Jesse kicked and screeched as Mayumi openly wept, negating any calming effect of Lemuel's voice. "Let him go!" she cried.

Rojas released the alpaca and he bolted from the barn and into the field, barely half shorn and lopsided.

"Give me a minute," she said, wiping her cheek with a sleeve. Her watch pinged with a call from Arturo. As much as she wanted to talk with her son, the call was dismissed. She didn't want him stressing over her voice cracking with emotion. The shearing had to be done. Buyers were waiting. Mayumi scanned the pen through tears that blurred the beasts awaiting their turn. "Bring Maria. She's always easy."

**To continue reading, visit Shoreline of Infinity Supplemental at:**

www.shorelineofinfinity.com/31-supplemental/

# my Pet

## Flash fiction competition for Shoreline of Infinity Readers

Bring the pet of your **science fictional** imagination to life. You have 1,000 words to tell its story. You may begin.

### Prizes

£50 for the winning story, plus 1-year digital subscription to *Shoreline of Infinity*. Two runners-up will each receive a 1-year digital subscription to Shoreline of Infinity.

The top three stories will be published in the December issue *Shoreline of Infinity* – all three finalists will receive a print copy of this edition.

### The detail

Maximum 1,000 words, one story per submitter.

The story must not have been previously published.

*Deadline for entries: midnight (UK time) 2nd September 2022.*

*To enter, visit the website at:*

*www.shorelineofinfinity.com/2022ffc*

*There's no entry fee, but on the submission entry form on the website you will be asked to enter a particular word from this issue of Shoreline of Infinity, so have it ready by your side when you submit.*

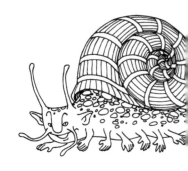

Lightning Source UK Ltd.
Milton Keynes UK
UKHW021352250522
403506UK00010B/1585